Orcus Child

Hell's Children Book 2

Molly Neely

Orcus Child

Published by:
Cloaked Press, LLC
PO Box 341
Suring, WI 54174
Cloakedpress.com

Cover Design by: Carmilla M. Ravensworth
Carmilla M. Ravensworth (carmillacreates.carrd.co)

Paperback ISBN: 978-1-952796-25-8

Dedication

Because of you, my life has been filled with meaning and purpose. You inspire me, support me and complete me. Even if I live a thousand years, it still won't be enough time to tell you how much I love you. My best friend. My husband.

CONTENTS

Chapter One...1

Chapter Two..5

Chapter Three..11

Chapter Four..15

Chapter Five..21

Chapter Six...25

Chapter Seven...29

Chapter Eight...35

Chapter Nine..39

Chapter Ten...45

Chapter Eleven...51

Chapter Twelve..59

Chapter Thirteen..61

Chapter Fourteen 65

Chapter Fifteen...73

Chapter Sixteen..79

Chapter Seventeen..85

Chapter Eighteen..91

Chapter Nineteen 95

Chapter Twenty...101

Chapter Twenty-One 107

Chapter Twenty-Two 113

Chapter Twenty-Three...117

Chapter Twenty-Four...123

Chapter Twenty-Five..125

Chapter Twenty-Six 129

Chapter Twenty-Seven 135

Chapter Twenty-Eight 141

Chapter Twenty-Nine 147

Chapter Thirty 151

Chapter Thirty-One 153

Chapter Thirty-Two 159

Chapter Thirty-Three 165

Chapter Thirty-Four 167

Chapter Thirty-Five 173

Chapter Thirty-Six 177

Chapter Thirty-Seven 181

Chapter Thirty-Eight 189

Chapter Thirty-Nine 195

Chapter Forty 201

Chapter Forty-One 207

Chapter Forty-Two 209

Chapter Forty-Three 215

Acknowledgments 219

CHAPTER ONE

May, 1591, The Mohawk River

Akhila stepped lightly onto the water logged shore that separated the receding river from the land. Red, pasty earth squished up between her bare toes, its smooth texture a welcome change from the weeks of wearing shoes. The rains had finally come to a close days earlier and now the sun was calling one and all to come out into the light.

She took a deep breath, savoring the sweet scents left behind on the hickory leaves and sycamore trees that lined the Mohawk River. She stripped off the rest of her clothes and tossed them absently into a nearby cluster of bushes. Clad only with a simple strand of beads around her neck the young Akwesasne teen waded out into the frigid water, anxious to wash away the dust of confinement.

The sun smiled down on her. Akhila spread her arms out and leaned back, allowing the water to cradle her. As she floated down the river, songs from the birds penetrated the rumblings of the river, a serenade that kept in time with the current and lulled her into a dreamy trance.

A stirring in the distance snapped her back to reality. With both hands, Akhila cleared away the water from her eyes then scanned river for the source of the noise. A few yards ahead, in the midst of a cluster of rocks. Akhila spied a giant salmon, thrashing against the current. Its massive head and long, shimmering body came up out of the water. Then like a breaching whale, the fish came down hard on the water's surface, over and over.

She watched for a few moments, unsure what the animal was doing. It soon became clear; the great fish was struggling. Instinctively, she began to swim towards it. As she grew closer, the salmon stopped thrashing.

"What is it, River Father?" Akhila asked softly, stroking the fish along its back. "Why do you fight against the waters?"

The salmon leaned his head against her hand. Akhila caressed the creatures head, then with her other hand she reached down and scratched his belly. The fish responded with a nudge of his nose. Then he lifted his head out of the water and peered into her eyes. There in the great fish's gaze she saw it. A cry for help.

Akhila felt around in the water. After a few moments of blind searching, she discovered the trouble.

"Poor River Father," Akhila cried. "Your tail is caught in these rocks!"

Akhila took a deep breath and went under. Through a vale of air bubbles and sediment, she could see the salmon's tail had wedged between two large stones. Gently, she grasped the tail with both hands, then carefully slid it up and out from between them. Released from its prison, the salmon quickly disappeared beneath the current.

As Akhila came back up to the surface, the fish doubled back and began circling her.

"Is there something else I can do for you?" Akhila asked.

The salmon once again dove under the water. With its powerful mouth, the fish grabbed hold of Akhila's leg and began to drag her down river, towards the open ocean.

CHAPTER TWO

November 1591, Kent

The metallic clang of the brass door knocker vibrated through the downstairs rooms. Malachi glanced up from the book in his lap, eyeing Reginald with suspicion.

"Are you expecting visitors?" he asked.

"No," Reginald replied sipping his tea.

A few minutes later, a more delicate knock sounded at the library door, then silently opened.

"What is it, Alice dear?" Reginald said. "Who was that at the door?"

His wife Alice Scot strode across the room, a small plain box tucked under her arm.

"A delivery boy left this at the door," she answered, handing Malachi the box. "It is addressed to you, Malachi."

Both men jerked upright in their leather chairs, their eyes locked on each other with nervous fear. It had been over a month since the two of them had hastily left Scotland. And while Reginald was free to move about in the open, Malachi was on a self-imposed house arrest.

"I do not understand," Malachi stuttered, "no one knows that I am here."

Reginald leaned forward and set down his cup. "Well,

obviously, someone does. Open it up my boy, or the suspense will surely kill me."

Malachi rolled his eyes. Then he untied the simple jute twine and cautiously lifted off the self-imposed lid. His heart froze in his chest, as he pulled out a neatly folded letter and Balthazar's half charred leather journal.

"My God," Reginald whispered, "Is that what I think it is?"

"Yes," Malachi answered, turning the small book over in his hands. "Balthazar's notes. I thought this was destroyed in the bonfire."

With his thumb, Malachi fanned through the pages. He smiled. Nearly every page was intact. Absently, he reached up and clutched the pendant around his neck. "My brother, your work has survived the wrath of the sun god."

"Yes, but how?" Reginald asked. "And by who's hand?"

Malachi set the journal down on the small table beside his chair, then turned his attention to the note. "Perhaps this will explain."

He broke the simple wax seal and opened up the letter.

Malachi,

I fear the tides may soon turn against you, my son. The circumstances that caused you to flee Scotland have triggered events and could no doubt lead to your doom. I have salvaged this journal for your use, as it contains information you may need. While it is forbidden for me to reveal the future, I can aide you in battling the forces that seek to put their foot upon your neck in the present. I would have delivered it in person, but I am sure you would agree, that would not be the best of ideas.

Burn this letter. No one must know of the gift I have given you. Lucifer would simply not understand. Be always on guard, and beware of the treachery that lies in a woman's heart. It is a trap even they do not understand. Hell truly hath no fury.

—A

Malachi felt the blood drain from his face.

"Well?" Reginald whispered. "Who is the author?"

"I uh… it is…" Malachi stammered, his eyes darting from Alice to Reginald.

Reginald waved his hand at his wife. "My dear, if you please. Leave us."

Alice nodded, her face filled with worry. "Yes, of course. I shall be upstairs if you need me."

"Now then," he said, leaning forward. "Who wrote the note?"

"My father," Malachi replied, handing him the note. "My *real* father, Azazael."

Reginald took the note and leaned back in his chair. Carefully, he read the letter, taking in every word. When he had finished reading, Reginald stood up, walked to the fireplace and tossed it in. The smoldering coals ignited the parchment instantly, sending flames of gold, green and purple shooting up the chimney. With one hand buried in his vest pocket, Reginald leaned against the mantle.

"Well, there you have it."

Malachi cocked his head. "What?"

"You have been cooped up here for a month, with no clue as to your next move. Now you know there are plots against you." Reginald replied. "I think you had better begin studying that journal."

"Yes, but," Malachi began.

"No buts," Reginald snapped back. "I will ring for some late supper and a bottle of wine. We need to discover what secrets Balthazar hid in that book. There's a reason Ra wanted it destroyed."

Malachi looked down at the pendant still clutched in his hand. The sorrow in his heart pulsed and burned. He thought back to the day Uphir had changed his friend. He remembered the warning. Balthazar's body had been destroyed by the fire, but his soul—

"His soul!" he bellowed, lurching forward in his chair.

Reginald jumped at the sudden outburst. "Soul? Who's soul?"

Malachi grabbed the journal off the table and frantically began flipping through the pages.

"His body was consumed by the fire, but his *soul* is still in the pendant."

"What does that have to do with your enemies in hell?" Reginald asked.

"If I figured it out," Malachi said, "it will only be a matter of time before Ra and Zilpah figure it out. As long as Balthazar's soul is in this curse tablet, they can still exact revenge on him. There has got to be something in this journal we can use to set his spirit free."

"There you go, my boy!" Reginald said, clapping his hands. "It is time for action. But, wars are not won on an empty stomach."

Reginald jerked on a long woven cord that hung near the door. A few moments later, a shy servant walked in carrying a silver tray and a bottle of wine. She set everything down on a buffet near the library's only window, then slipped out of sight.

For the next hour, the two sat in silence, picking at a rack of lamb and boiled potatoes the servant had left. With greasy fingers, Malachi scoured the journal, and quickly found that the dove merchant had been exceedingly thorough in his notes. Every possible cure for Malachi's curse had been documented, sorted by country of origin, and included extensive lists of contacts, rituals, recipes and even detailed maps.

"Any luck?" Reginald asked, pouring himself another glass of port. "You have been silent as the grave for over an hour."

Malachi sighed, rolling his shoulders. He balanced the journal on his knee, then leaned his head back and rested it on the back of his chair.

"No, nothing. Every page pertains to my curse. Nothing about his."

Reginald shook his head in defiance. "Do not lose heart. There has to be something you missed. We have all the time in the world. Keep looking."

"I am telling you, it is hopeless," Malachi snapped, standing up. The journal slipped off his knee and landed with a thud at his feet. As he reached down to pick it up, he noticed a small piece of parchment sticking out from between the unused pages.

"What do we have here?" Malachi asked, pulling the stray paper from the book.

Reginald leaned over and watched as Malachi unfolded it. In Balthazar's ragged hand was one line:

When my brother is cured, we go to Orcus.

"What does it say?" Reginald asked, taking a gulp of wine.

Malachi looked up, his hopeful gaze meeting Reginald's. "Do you have a book on Roman Mythology?"

CHAPTER THREE

"Says here, a temple to this Orcus fellow used to stand on Vatican Hill," Reginald mumbled. "I doubt it is still there."

Malachi nodded, continuing to flip through a book of Italian history. They had been dissecting every volume related to Greek and Roman gods for what seemed like an eternity. Slowly, the mystery of who and where Orcus was began to emerge.

Reginald continued. "I mean after all, what Pope in his right mind would allow that?"

The tinkling of chimes floated through the room as the clock above the mantle struck three am, followed by a faint knock at the door.

"Enter," Reginald called out, his eyes never leaving the text he was reading.

A sleep deprived maid tip-toed in carrying another tray. She stepped around several stacks of books and weaved her way to the buffet. There she swapped out the empty supper dishes for a large plate of fruit and a few wedges of cheese. Then she began to address the piles of discarded books.

"Oh bloody hell," Reginald barked to himself.

Malachi looked up from what he was reading. "What is it?"

"This is ridiculous," he replied. "All references to

Orcus point to rural cults tucked away in old faded villages. Not only is Orcus the god of the underworld, but it is also the name of the underworld. But of course none of these damn books can tell me if there are any temples left."

"Beggin' yer pardon sir," the servant piped in.

Reginald cleared his throat then slammed the book shut. "Yes, what is it?"

"Ifin' yer lookin' for Orcus, I knows how to gets there," she answered.

Both Reginald and Malachi stared at the servant in disbelief.

Reginald offered her a questioning glare.

"What do you mean, *you* know how to get there?"

The servant quickly curtsied. "Well sir, I—"

"What is your name, girl?" Reginald interrupted.

The nervous maid offered a quick curtsy while staring down at the floor. "Nancy sir, I am the downstairs maid, sir."

Reginald waved his hand at her. "Very well, Nancy, the downstairs maid, enlighten me. How do I find Orcus?"

"You see sir, I was thinkin' of joinin' a convent," Nancy began, "me mum sent me to Italy for two weeks. Twas all the money she had, sir. Anyways, I decided being a nun just wernt for me. So I did a bit of site-seein' if you will."

Malachi rolled his eyes in frustration. "At some point will your fascinating story tell us about Orcus?"

"Oh yes sir," Nancy blurted out. "Sees, I went to a town called Bomarzo. They gots a place there called 'Monsters Grove'. There in the gardens is a stone carving of giant 'ead, with stairs leadin' up to its mouth. A man I met there told me it twas the gateway to taws the land of the dead."

Reginald ran his hand across the stubble forming on his chin. He stood up and walked to the buffet. Mumbling to himself, he piled chunks of cheese and bread on a plate, grabbed up the bottle of wine, then returned to his chair. He poured himself a glass, took a bite of the cheese, then handed off the plate to Malachi.

"And how long ago were you in Bomarzo, Nancy?" he asked.

"Oh, twas just last year, sir." she replied. "When I gots back to England I gots this job, on a counta I spent all me mum's money."

Malachi chuckled under his breath, then took a bite of bread. "Reginald, Bomarzo is only about a day's journey from the Vatican. Perhaps the new Pope—"

"Would like a visit from a member of Parliament," Reginald finished. "Yes, that is an excellent idea. And while we are there, we can peruse the library, and see if there is any more information on this Orcus fellow."

"To Rome, then?" Malachi asked.

Reginald reached over and grabbed his glass. "To Rome."

CHAPTER FOUR

May, 1591, The Atlantic Ocean

There was no way to know for sure how far she had traveled. The salmon towed Akhila by the leg for what seemed like hours. But once they had reached the sea, the fish let go, opting instead for Akhila to simply hold on to his tail, while he took her further out into the open ocean.

"Where are we going, River Father?" Akhila had called out. "Why have you taken me so far from my home?"

The salmon stopped swimming. For several minutes, he simply circled Akhila while she tread water. Her eyes darted around in all directions, but she could no longer see land. She reached out and stroked the salmon's back as he passed by her.

"I wish you could talk," she shouted, "I wish you could tell me why we are here."

The fish disappeared again under the waves. Akhila looked around, frantically searching the dark churning water for her strange companion.

"Wait," she cried out, "River Father! Do not leave me behind!"

Suddenly, a mouth enclosed her calf and once again Akhila was pulled down into the blackened sea. She looked up and watched the sun fade into darkness as the fish pulled her deeper and deeper into the depths of the ocean. Akhila's lungs began to weaken as the quick gulp of air she took lost its potency. Her eyes burned from the salt. A heaviness settled in her head. The urge to take a breath was overwhelming. Akhila succumbed to the ocean, her conscious self disappearing into a current of oblivion.

***

"Arise my lady," a voice called out.

Akhila sat up, her eyes darting around the room. "Who is there?"

She rubbed the sleep from her face then drank in the new surroundings. The room was furnished with brightly colored corals, peppered with sea anemone who seemed to sway in time to some silent music carried on the current. Schools of clown fish darted in and out of the coral, picking bits of algae from its surface. In one corner of the room rested the salmon, calmly hovering a few inches from the sandy floor, watching her.

A large manta ray arose from the sand. It twisted and stretched into the shape of a human man. Then five angel fish swam into the room. They formed a ring around the man's head, swimming in a circle like a living crown.

"I see you are awake," the man said. "That is good. Your friend was worried you would not survive the journey."

"Who are you?" Akhila marveled.

"I am Poseidon," he replied, his voice booming like thunder. "God of the Sea. Of earthquakes and storms, I am he who churns the oceans and swirls the clouds into a frenzy! You are Akwesasne. Akhila, of the Flint Place."

A proud smile spread across Akhila's face. "You know of my people?" she asked.

"Indeed I do," Poseidon answered. "They are a grand and talented nation. You honor me with your presence. I understand you saved my beloved salmon yesterday."

Akhila blushed. "I only freed his tail from some rocks."

"A simple act of kindness can ring out like a thousand bells," Poseidon replied. "My beloved friend is eternally grateful, and wishes to never leave your side."

"I do not understand," Akhila said, "I am afraid there are a great many things I do not understand."

Poseidon cocked his head, "What is it you wish to be made clear, young lady?"

Akhila took a deep breath. "Well, how is it that I can breathe? Are we not at the ocean floor?"

"Yes, we are," Poseidon replied. "But my realm is filled with Olympian magic. If I wish for you to breathe, then you breathe. But do not fear, I will not hurt you, Akhila, of the Flint Place, you are here to be rewarded for your kindness."

Akhila slipped off the slab of cushioned coral she was sitting on and stood before the god. With her arms down at her sides, she gazed up into Poseidon's face, a proud and brave Akwesasne woman.

"Thank you," she said. "I accept whatever gift you see fit to give me."

Poseidon stroked his long white beard and smiled. "As you wish, my lady."

A faint chatter echoed into the coral room. Then from an opening in the ceiling, a great bottle nosed dolphin descended, carrying in its mouth a shiny golden trident. The beast gently placed the trident in Poseidon's outstretched hand, then swam away.

The salmon moved away from the corner he was resting in and joined Akhila in the center of the room.

Poseidon raised the trident above his head. "Akhila, I bind you to this beast, body and spirit for all time. He will take on your strength. You will take on his. Let the two, become one!"

Then he pointed the head of the trident directly at Akhila and the salmon. A blast of white light shot out from the weapon, engulfing her and the salmon. Like liquid smoke, millions of tiny bubbles filled the coral room. Within moments, the underwater cloud funneled out through the open ceiling.

When Akhila opened her eyes. The salmon was gone.

"Where is he?" she cried, scanning the room. "What has happened to him?"

Poseidon let out a great belly laugh. "My lady, look upon yourself! He is a part of you now."

Akhila looked down and let out a shriek. Her hips and legs were gone, replaced with a long, silvery fish tail. She ran her hands down the length of her new tail, feeling the texture of the scales. Her eyes welled up with tears as she glanced back up at Poseidon.

"Please do not think I am ungrateful," she cried, "but does this mean I am bound to the water? Will I never see my people again?"

"Of course you will," Poseidon replied. "The great

salmon must travel up river every year. So shall you. When the urge to spawn comes upon you, during that time you will be free to change your form at will. And in time, you will not have to wait for the spawning season. But like the salmon, when the urge leaves you, to the sea you must return."

Akhila nodded. "I understand."

"You will soon see what a treasured gift this is," Poseidon said. "There are many strange and wondrous powers that come with it. In time, you will master them all. Now go, explore your new world, Akhila, Mermaid of the Flint Place."

Chapter Five

January 2nd, 1592, Venice Italy

The weeks leading up to the trip to Italy had been slow and mundane. Malachi stewed in anticipation, while Reginald made all the arrangements for travel. His anxiety grew even stronger while aboard the merchant ship bound for Venice. Malachi would have preferred their destination to have been closer to Rome, but the short notice caused beggars to not be so choosy. As the ship docked in the port, Malachi slung his bag over his shoulder, and made his way down the gang plank. It was his first visit to 'The Floating City', and already his senses were on high alert.

"My word, this is a strange town," Reginald commented, stepping off the wooden plank. "But that is exactly why it is perfect for our needs."

"Really?" Malachi raised an eyebrow. "How so?"

"The residents of Venice are much more open minded than other parts of Italy," Reginald answered. "We will have a lot more freedom to ask questions here than in other parts of the country. That is why I didn't quibble about coming here when my valet told me this was the only passage he could get us in such short notice."

Malachi nodded. "I see. So where do we go from here?"

Reginald pointed to a stuccoed building in front of them. "To the harbor master, I suppose. He should be able put us in touch with the proper contacts."

The two walked to the harbor master's office. The room was simple, a desk in the center, with a burly, bearded man seated behind it. He looked up and offered a half smile.

"Parli Italiano?"

Reginald stepped forward and cleared his throat. "Em, no, English, per favore."

The harbor master gave a snort. "English," he muttered, shaking his head. "What can I do for you gentlemen?"

"We have just come ashore," Reginald began, "and are looking to make some arrangements for travel. We need to go to Rome, and Bomarzo."

"What is your business in Rome, Signore?"

"You see, I am Reginald Scot, a member of the English Parliament, and my companion and I would like to visit with the Pope."

Shaking his head, the harbor master replied. "Not possible, Signore."

"Of all the insolence," Reginald shouted, "In heaven's name why not?"

"I am sorry to tell you, Signore, the Pope is dead. Died last month." He paused a moment and crossed himself.

"Since you were at sea when it happened, I can understand why you would not know."

Stunned, Reginald turned and stared at Malachi, his mouth agape. The Vatican would be in an uproar trying to find a new Pope. There was no way they would be allowed in now.

"Well," Malachi grumbled, "do we have a plan B?"

"Signore, you can still arrange for transport to Bomarzo," the harbor master answered. "I will set you up with a place to sleep, and send a man over in the morning to make the arrangements."

"That would be satisfactory," Reginald said, offering a slight bow. "Thank you for the information."

"Very good, Signore." the harbor master said. "Marco!"

A door opened at the far end of the room. A young boy, no older than twelve rushed in.

"Si, papa?" the boy asked.

"Prendere questi uomini alla locanda," he answered.

Marco nodded without a word, and began gathering up Malachi and Reginald's bags.

"My son will take you to your lodgings. It is not far from here." the harbor master said. "Good luck to you."

Chapter Six

alachi wandered around the room, inspecting the elaborate decor of their rooms. Thick red velvet draperies tied with gold cords hung from the windows, clashing and yet not with the intricately embroidered purple and blue cushions piled on the over-stuffed beds. Plush carpets layered one on top of the other, covered the floor in a desperate attempt to mask the creaking planks. He stopped at a gaudy oil painting hanging near the door. With a disapproving glare, he removed it from its hook and sat it down, facing the wall.

"I take it over fed, naked women lounging on a bed of cherubs is not your idea of art?" Reginald said with a snort. "After all these centuries, you sir are still a prude and a snob."

Malachi rolled his eyes. "I cannot help it. After all, I am an ancient Jew. Even you have to admit, this room looks more like a brothel than a inn."

"Quite right," Reginald agreed, "but when in Venice..."

"You sound like Balthazar," Malachi said with a nod. "He would be looking for a way to make money off this room."

"Indeed, he would," Reginald said with a sigh. "You know..."

"What is it?" Malachi asked.

Reginald sat down on the edge of one of the beds. "I have never expressed to you how truly sorry I am for your loss. Call it a shortcoming on my part. I can only imagine the grief you have been going through all these weeks, and I should have done more to ease your burden."

Malachi walked to the open window and looked out at the canal below. In the two months since Balthazar's death, he hadn't allowed himself to think about it. There hadn't been time to. As he watched the gondolas creep past on the water, Malachi was suddenly overwhelmed with sorrow.

"I miss his voice," he whispered. "I miss his insane logic and his justification for doing the most ridiculous things. I miss my nerves being on edge every time he opened his mouth, for fear we would get arrested. It never occurred to me that I would ever lose him."

Reginald stood up and joined him at the window. "I may not be much of a replacement, but you will always have my allegiance and my friendship."

Malachi turned and faced Reginald. "No person can replace another. I value you just as I value the many humans that have been in my life. You are a true friend, Reginald."

The two stood silently for a few moments, taking in the salt air that wafted in through the window. A calmness settled in Malachi's chest, as he allowed the magic of Venice to overshadow him. Then like the thunder before a storm, a knock at the door broke the spell.

"Enter, er a, *entrare!*" Reginald called out.

A young woman in a simple gray dress opened the door. She walked across the room, her strides tinkling from a delicate strand of bells that encircled her ankle. Without a word, she handed Reginald a note.

"Signore, questo e venuto per voi," she said in a mousy voice.

Reginald took the note. "Grazie,"

The woman nodded, then offered Malachi a brief smile before quickly leaving the room.

"What is it?" Malachi asked.

Reginald sighed. "Seems we have been invited to dinner,"

CHAPTER SEVEN

"Da questa parte, Signore," the servant girl said, answering the door. "Il maestro si unira a voi a breve."

The same shy messenger that delivered the invitation earlier, led Malachi and Reginald through the house to a small, secluded patio garden. As she opened the glass doors that led outside, a cool breeze floated in, catching the scent of her perfume. The young girl stole a glance at Malachi. He met her gaze with a warm smile, then took a deep breath, inhaling her sweet, and floral scent. Embarrassed at being discovered, the girl quickly looked away, her ears flush with red. She gathered a silver tray from a cubbyhole in the wall, loaded with crystal glasses, a bottle of wine, a cluster of deep purple grapes and a large pile of figs. Silently and efficiently the servant set the simple bistro style table, then motioned for Malachi and Reginald to sit down.

"Si prega di avere un po'di vino," she said, motioning to the wine and fruit. "do palease halp yoursalf."

Malachi chuckled under his breath. "Grazie, mio caro," he replied.

The young girl blushed again, then hurried back into the house, leaving behind only faint traces of her perfume and the distant tinkling of bells.

Reginald poured himself a hefty glass and sat down.

"I do believe you have bewitched that girl," he said. "Perhaps she would like to go with us to Bomarzo."

Malachi snorted loudly. "She would die of nervousness before we even left the city. Poor beautiful thing. She will make someone a very good wife one day."

"If you mean Lucette, my servant, you would be right, Signore," a voice quipped behind him.

Malachi turned and saw an elderly gentleman standing there.

"She is a kind and gentle soul," the old man continued, "Lucette has been in my employ for only a short time, but already I would be lost in this house without her."

Reginald stood up and gave a slight bow. "Good evening, Sir. I am Reginald Scot, this is my companion, Malachi Ben Sinai. We are honored to be invited to the home of the Doge of Venice."

The old Doge extended his hand. "The honor is mine, Signore. We do not stand on formalities here. Per favore, call me Pasquale."

Reginald took his hand and shook it warmly. "Quite right, and please, do call me Reginald."

Pasquale released Reginald's hand and pulled out a chair at the bistro. Then he sat down, releasing a long, winded sigh as his old bones settled into the cast iron seat. He poured himself three fingers of wine, took a long swig from the glass, then sighed again.

"What a day," he said, refilling the glass. "It gets harder and harder as the years go by. Malachi il mio regazzo, do not ever grow old. It is hell on the body."

Malachi flashed a knowing smile at Reginald, then sat down beside the Doge. "I will try and remember that,

Signore,"

"Tell me, Reginald," Pasquale continued, "what brings you to Venice? I was surprised when little Marco came and told me a member of British Parliament was here. I had no time to plan the usual fanfare."

"That certainly would not have been necessary," Reginald replied. "We are simply passing through. Hoping actually, to obtain transportation to Bomarzo tomorrow."

Pasquale nodded. "Ah, Bomarzo, a lovely place. They have a beautiful garden there called the Monsters Grove."

Malachi and Reginald looked at each other and smiled.

"What a coincidence that you should mention the gardens," Malachi said, pinching off a handful of grapes from the tray. "That is where we were planning to go."

"Because you are seeking the entrance to Orcus."

The mention of Orcus startled Malachi. He began choking on a mouthful of fruit.

Pasquale reached over and gave him a few firm pats on the back, dislodging the half-chewed food.

"For heaven's sake il mio ragazzo," Pasquale said, pouring Malachi a glass of wine. "Are you alright?"

Malachi took a drink of wine. "Yes, thank you. I was just a little surprised."

"What he means is…" Reginald began.

The old doge put up his hand. "I know what he means. He did not think I knew about the entrance to Orcus." Pasquale paused and looked directly into Malachi's eyes. "Did you, demon?"

Reginald jumped to his feet. "Now, see here—"

"Ah, mio amico, have no fear," Pasquale said, his gaze still focused on Malachi. "I knew what he was before the two of you even arrived. I have been expecting him for over a month."

Malachi frowned deeply. "Over a month? What do you mean? Has Ra been here to see you?"

"Whoever that is, I do not know," Pasquale replied. "No, my last visitor was a most mysterious and beautiful woman."

Malachi shook his head as anger and unwanted desire swelled in his belly. The old Doge could only be referring to one woman.

"What did she want?"

Pasquale leaned back in his chair. "She asked if a handsome Jewish man had been in the city, inquiring about ancient lore. She described you perfectly, il mio rigazzo, including who and *what* you are. This woman wanted me to inform her the moment you arrived in Venice."

"And what did you say to that?" Malachi asked, leaning forward.

"I explained to la donna, that I had no intention of getting involved in a lovers intrigue."

Malachi rolled his eyes in disgust. "We are not lovers," he mumbled.

"She pressed me no further, il mio ragazzo," Pasquale said, "she just simply left."

"My God," Reginald exclaimed. "Zilpah. But, that is impossible. We watched her die!"

"You mean, we *thought* we watched her die," Malachi growled under his breath.

"Blast it all!" Reginald shouted. "We should just call this whole thing off. What chance have we, when the hounds of hell are at our heels?"

As Reginald paced back and forth, Malachi's mind began to race. *Was Zilpah really here*, he wondered. The idea terrified him, and yet the memory of their last encounter sent butterflies leaping in his belly. Though the spell she had cast on him was long broken, the affect had left its mark There was a part of him that remained bewitched.

Malachi took a long pull off his wine glass and tried to stay focused.

"Sit down, Reginald," he said calmly. "Do not let her get inside your head."

"Your companion is right, Signore," Pasquale said. "Whatever your purpose is here, do not be swayed by dark forces. If God is for you, there is no force that can stand against you."

Reginald nodded slowly, his lips pursed tightly. He sat back down and grabbed his glass.

"You are quite right," he replied. Then he turned and faced Malachi. "What do you want to do?"

"Well," Malachi began, "she must have given up. Otherwise she'd still be in the city. I say we continue on to Bomarzo as planned."

"Molto bravo!" Pasquale cheered, clapping his hands twice. "Now, let us celebrate with a meal."

Lucette returned to the patio, her hands loaded with trays of assorted grilled meats & fish, vegetables, and risotto.

"Do not worry about a thing, il mio ragazzo," Pasquale said grabbing a chunk of fish from one of the trays. "In the morning, I will arrange for a carriage to take you to Bomarzo. It is about a four day journey. But, you will see countryside that is il piu bello. Eh, that is to say, some of the most lovely in all the world."

Lucette leaned over Malachi's shoulder and set a plate of roasted shellfish in front of him. Once again her sweet scent reached his nose. He turned his head slightly, his face just inches from hers and inhaled deeply. Lucette gazed at him from the corner of her eye, then quickly looked away. Her determined shyness was almost intoxicating.

He reached out and gently took Lucette's hand.

"Molto bello," he said, with a playful wink.

Lucette's face bloomed pure crimson. "Grazie," she replied, in a mousy whisper. "Thank you vary mach, Signore."

Then she pulled away and slipped out of the garden, while the doge and his guests got down to the business of eating.

Reginald let loose a chuckle and drained his glass.

"When we return from Bomarzo, I think you should marry that girl."

CHAPTER EIGHT

November, 1591, The Mohawk River

Bonsari wiped away the streaks of tears from her cheeks. Staring out at the river as it rushed by, her mind fought against the anxiety of a single unanswered question. Where was Akhila? Her eldest daughter, the light of her life, had vanished from river bank nearly six months earlier. The only trace of her that had remained, were the clothes she was wearing when she left that morning.

Absently, Bonsari reached up and ran her finger tips along her necklace, a simple strand of beads. Akhila had been wearing a similar strand the day she disappeared. Mother and daughter had made them together, each wearing the others as a gesture of love and deep affection. Bonsari sniffed back another tear. She feared the worst. The beads were all that remained of her beautiful child.

"Please give her back to me," she called out to the water. "If you have taken my Akhila, please, give her back."

The steady rush of the current was the river's only reply. Bonsari turned her back to the Mohawk. The same river she came to every day, with her heart full of hope. The same river she would plead with to return her child. But the water never answered her question. Where is

Akhila? Perhaps it was time to let her go. Even Bonsari's own husband, a skilled hunter and tracker, had said it was time.

"Momma?" a voice called out from the current.

Bonsari whipped back around and stumbled to the edge of the water.

"Akhila?"

"Yes, Momma!" the voice shouted again.

With her heart leaping out of her chest, Bonsari waded out into the water, her eyes scanning up and down.

"Where are you my child?" she called out, the water now up to her chest. "I cannot see you,"

A gentle hand touched her shoulder. "I am here."

Bonsari turned and found herself face to face with her long-lost daughter. She flung her arms around the girl and pulled her close. Over and over she stroked Akhila's hair, while planting kisses on her cheeks.

"My beautiful child," Bonsari whispered, "I was afraid the river would never let you come home."

"But, how did you know?" Akhila asked.

"Your father could only find tracks going into the river, but none coming out," Bonsari replied. "We knew only that the water had consumed you. Where have you been all this time?"

Akhila looked away for a moment. "It will be hard to explain."

"What do you mean?" her mother asked. "Do not be afraid to tell me."

"It would be better if I showed you," Akhila said, pulling away from her mother's embrace. "Do not be afraid Momma, I have been given a wondrous gift."

Akhila slowly backed away from her mother, moving out to the deepest part of the river. Then without warning, she sunk down into the water, disappearing from view.

Bonsari was suddenly struck with panic.

"Akhila?" she yelled, "Akhila!"

Then like a dolphin in open water, Akhila launched out of the river, her silver tail gleaming in the sun like the stars in a night sky. Gracefully, she reentered the water, a perfect breech, with hardly a splash.

Bonsari's mouth hung open.

Akhila broke the surface again and swam to her mother.

"What has happened to you?" Bonsari asked.

"I saved the life of a great salmon," Akhila said, pointing at a spot in the water a few feet away. "Right there. He took me from the river, out into the open ocean. I met a god there, named Poseidon."

"Poseidon?" Bonsari asked with a frown. "I have not heard of this god."

Akhila nodded. "He says he is the ruler over all the seas. He told me the salmon was grateful that I saved his life and never wanted to be parted from me. And so I am now bound to it for all time."

Worry washed over Bonsari's face. "So you and the salmon—"

"Are one." Akhila replied, "body and spirit."

Bonsari hung her head, turned and began to make her way to the shore. A small tear welled in the corner of her eye. As she stepped out of water, the tear began to crawl down her cheek. With a shaking hand, Bonsari absently wiped it away.

"Momma!" Akhila called out, swimming towards the river's edge. "Wait for me."

Bonsari turned and looked back at her daughter.

"Why?" she said. "You belong to the waters now."

Beneath the current, Akhila could feel her tail split in two. The water around her churned and groaned, as its hold on Akhila's human half was severed from its liquid control. The scaly exterior of her skin began to soften as the color changed from silver to bronze. Once naked and mortal, Akhila stepped onto the shore of the Mohawk River, with two legs.

Bonsari dropped to her knees and grasped at her daughter's smooth ankles. She ran her hands up and down Akhila's legs, then looked up into her daughters smiling face.

"But, you said for all time."

"Yes," Akhila said, helping her mother to her feet. "And like the River Father, I must spawn every year. Poseidon says during the spawning, I can change back and be with my people."

Bonsari threw her arms around her daughter and held her tight.

"Oh my beautiful child," she whispered in Akhila's ear. "Your father will be so happy. Come, let us go home."

CHAPTER NINE

January 3rd, 1592, Venice Italy

The sun peaked out shyly from the tops of the buildings that lined the canal. Morning had arrived in Venice. Malachi sat up slowly in his bed and gazed out the open window. Warm rays streamed in, bringing life to his tired limbs. He raised his arms over his head and stretched. Then glanced at the sleeping statesman that snored next to him.

"Reginald," he whispered, giving the old aristocrat an elbow. "Reginald, it is morning. We need to prepare for our journey."

Reginald groaned under the bedclothes and rolled over.

"Why do I feel as though I only just went to bed? And why does my head feel like I have been trampled by horses?"

"Because we have only been in our room since before dawn," Malachi snorted, throwing back the covers and standing up. "My word, can that old man drink!"

Reginald sat up and swung his legs over the side of the bed. He let out a great yawn then reached for his trousers.

"Quite right," he said, "the Doge of Venice is the purest definition of 'eat, drink and be merry' I have ever seen."

"Do you think he will keep his word and arrange a carriage for us to Bomarzo?" Malachi asked.

A low knock at the door hummed through the morning air. Malachi looked at Reginald with a raised eyebrow.

"Hallo?" a muffled voice chimed through the door.

Malachi padded across the room and opened the door. There stood Lucette, who briefly drunk in an eyeful of his bare chest and legs, before letting out a squeal and turning pure crimson.

"Oh! Signore!" she whispered, staring at the floor. "Mi dispiace, perdonoami."

Malachi looked down at his barely dressed self and chuckled. "It is ok, sei perdonato. What can I do for you, mio caro?"

"The carriage is ready for you," Lucette replied. "Can I halp you with your baggage?"

"No, thank you, Lucette," Malachi answered.

Lucette nodded. Overcome by a burst of bravery, she grabbed Malachi by his shoulders and kissed him. The brazen act caused her face to blush all over again as she pulled away and took a step back.

"Signore," she said, staring down at the floor, "when your business is finished in Bomarzo, will you return to Venice?"

"I will," Malachi said, taking her hand. "Se solo per vederti."

A smile spread across Lucette's face. She nodded slightly then backed away.

"Bon viaggio," she said. "I will see you soon."

She turned and bolted down the hall, the flutters of

anticipation raising the hairs on her slender neck. When she reached the landing, Lucette pushed open the large heavy door that led to the street and stepped out into the warmth of the morning sun. He said he was coming back. If only to see *her*.

Lucette smoothed her skirt and began to walk back to the home of the Doge. She turned down an alley, paved with smooth cobblestones and darkened by the looming buildings that lined either side of the narrow walkway.

She heard the creak of a door open ahead of her. A dark woman in a deep blue dress, cinched tight with a black velvet bodice, stepped out into the alley and faced her.

"Are you the one they call Lucette?"

Lucette nodded. "Si, I am Lucette."

The woman held out her hand and motioned the servant girl over.

"Come here," the woman beckoned, "hai qualcosa di cui ho bisogno,"

"What is it that you want from me?" Lucette asked, inching closer.

The woman absently reached up and twirled a loose strand of black hair between her long and slender fingers.

"Information," the woman replied. "Did the Doge receive visitors from England last night?"

"Yes," Lucette answered. "A man from Parliament called Reginald Scot and—"

"And?" the woman pressed.

"There was a younger man named Malachi." Lucette answered with a smile.

"I see," the woman said, stepping closer. "Why did

they go see the Doge?"

Lucette could feel a nervous twitch brewing in her. She took a step back.

"I—"

The dark woman lunged, snatching Lucette by the arm. Then she twisted the arm around behind her back, while grabbing her firmly by the neck with her other hand. She pulled her close, pressing the frightened servant girl against her body. The scent of fear penetrated the woman's nose, filling her veins with endorphins and longing.

"I want to know why?" she growled in Lucette's ear.

"T-they wanted halp with travel," Lucette stuttered.

The woman tightened her grip on Lucette's neck. "Travel to where?"

"B-bomarzo," Lucette squeaked. "The Monster's Garden."

The woman smiled, revealing a pair of needle-sharp fangs. "Thank you, that is all I needed to know,"

Like a viper, the woman reared back and sank her teeth deep into the servant girl's neck. The blood flowed down her throat, its warmth reviving her muscles and energizing her senses. When Lucette's body had given up its last drop, the woman let go, allowing the dead girl to fall face down and drape across her feet like a rag doll.

"You are so selfish," a man whispered behind her.

The woman turned, absently primping the sleeves of her dress.

"Here," she said with a smile, rolling Lucette's body over with her foot. "Perhaps there is some left."

The man stepped out into the alley, carefully avoiding

the few rays of morning sun that managed to brighten the paving stones. With his face hidden beneath the oversized hood on his cloak, he eyed the body with a glint of hope in his belly. Then he knelt down and inhaled deep, searching for remnants of the girl's essence. His shoulders fell in disappointment. The only scent that remained was Lucette's perfume.

"There is none," he sighed, stroking the dead girl's hair. "Zilpah my pet, once again, your appetite knows no bounds."

"It could not be helped," Zilpah laughed. "She was delicious. And most helpful."

"Did she tell you where the half-breed was going?"

"Yes," Zilpah answered. "It seems the old Doge set him and the Englishman up with transportation to Bomarzo. Why would he want to go there?"

The man remained silent, still running his fingers through Lucette's hair.

"Ra?" she demanded. "Why would Malachi want to go to Bomarzo?"

The Sun god stood and straightened his coat, his eyes locked with hers. Ra reached out with his index finger and wiped away a stray drop of blood from the corner of Zilpah's mouth. His eyes never wavering, he suckled the drop from his finger, relishing the faint flavor of the dead girl at his feet.

"Because my pet, there is an entrance to the underworld in Bomarzo."

The rumble of carriage wheels and horse hooves echoed down the alley from the street. The two broke their gaze and looked on, as Malachi and Reginald's carriage passed by.

Ra reached out and gently caressed Zilpah's cheek.

"I cannot go with you, my dear," he said, "Lucifer has me sailing for some place called Korea. You will have to find out why the half-breed is trying to sneak into Hell all by yourself."

Chapter Ten

"Do you think man will ever figure out a way to make traveling easier?"

Malachi snorted and glanced out the window of the carriage. It had been a long and bumpy four days on the road to Bomarzo. As the sun reached high into noonday, the cramped and now smelly transportation had finally come to a stop.

"I suppose," Malachi chuckled, opening the carriage door. "It amazes me the things that man has been able to accomplish since I was born."

Both men stepped out of the carriage and stretched their legs.

"Yes well," Reginald sighed, "If you ask me, it is truly amazing that man has survived as long as he has."

Malachi and Reginald entered the Monster's Garden through the main gate, book ended by a pair of large, stone sphinxes. Reginald stopped, his gaze falling on an inscription carved into one of the stone giants.

"You who enter here,
consider what you are seeing
and tell me if so many
wonders are made by tricks
or by art"

"Tricks," Malachi mumbled.

Reginald laughed out loud. "Pessimist,"

They set out on a dirt trail, passing massive carved statues of turtles, winged horses and even Neptune himself. Leaves from the towering trees almost jingled like bells on the breeze, only to be drowned out by the rushing waters that tumbled over a nearby waterfall. Up ahead stood a house. A simple rectangular structure, made complicated by its leaning to one side.

"There," Malachi said, pointing beyond the house. "there's the entrance."

Amongst the great carvings of dragons, giants and wizards stood the entrance to Orcus. Set in a hill, it had a large carved face, its gaping mouth and flared nostrils pulled almost into a snarl. On its facade grew a layer of emerald green moss, while weeds and creeping grasses inched themselves up the stone steps that led to the entrance. The eyes were hollow and deep, never blinking and always watching. It was appropriately named, The Ogre.

As they stood at the base of the steps, Reginald could feel his hands go clammy and cold.

"Are you sure about this?"

Malachi smiled, giving Reginald a sideways glance.

"Do not tell me you are afraid?"

Reginald cleared his throat and straightened his coat.

"A bit nervous, perhaps," he replied. "I have never been inside a gateway to the underworld before."

The two began to ascend the steps. When they reached the top step, Reginald leaned back to get a better view of another inscription.

"Abandon all thought,
ye who enter here"

"See there," Reginald said, shaking an anxious finger at the inscription. "And you wonder why I have cause for concern."

Malachi shook his head and sighed.

"If you would rather wait in the carriage—"

"No, no!" Reginald replied, giving his coat another nervous yank. "I am no coward. Let us be off, then."

They stepped into the mouth of the ogre, allowing themselves to be swallowed by the darkness. Inside was nothing more than a large room, containing a simple table and two chairs in the center. The thick stone walls muffled the sounds coming off the rest of the gardens.

"It is as quiet as death in here," Reginald whispered.

Malachi nodded. "Yes it is."

"I must admit, now that we are here, I am a bit underwhelmed." Reginald continued.

"Hmmm,"

Malachi walked the perimeter of the room, dragging his fingertips along the wall. When he came to the south wall, Malachi suddenly pulled his hand away.

"What the devil is wrong, Malachi?" Reginald asked.

"What the devil, indeed," Malachi answered, beckoning his companion closer. "Here, feel this wall."

Reginald placed his palm on the carved stone, then immediately pulled away.

"Why, its hot!" he cried.

"I believe we have found it," Malachi said. "Now, how to get in—"

With both hands, Malachi began examining the wall.

"There must be a lever or door or something here,"

When he reached the center of the wall, his hands plunged through the stone, as if it were made of mist. Malachi jerked his hands back, the momentum sending him sprawling on the ground.

"D-did you see that?" he stammered, pulling himself back to his feet.

Reginald cautiously walked to the wall and pressed his hand against it.

"How did you do that?" he asked, pushing on the wall. "It is as solid as, well, stone."

"I do not know," Malachi answered, approaching the wall. "Perhaps because of my—"

"Special lineage?" Reginald winked.

Malachi shot him an irritated frown. "Ahem, yes,"

Reginald walked over and stood next to him. He gently placed a hand on Malachi's shoulder and gave it a fatherly squeeze.

"Well?"

Malachi turned to Reginald. "What?"

"Get on with it," Reginald said. "I'll wait for you in Venice as long as I can. If you are gone longer than I can stay, I will leave you some money with the Doge."

Malachi sniffed back a tear and patted Reginald's hand.

"I love you like a father, Lord Scot," he whispered. "You are a good man,"

"And I love you like a son," Reginald replied, "Now go, save your friend."

Malachi turned and faced the southern wall of the ogre. A wave of dread rippled through his body, settling in the pit of his guts. He wondered what horrors waited for him on the other side of the wall. Then shoving down the fear, Malachi took a deep breath and stepped through the invisible gate, disappearing into it like a ghost.

CHAPTER ELEVEN

January 8th, 1592, the Mohawk River

"**M**y heart is heavy, Akhila."

"I know," she replied.

"It is the wish of our parents that you and I—"

"Please, Tsio," Akhila cried, pressing her hand to his lips. "Do not break my heart anymore. I accepted a long time ago the path chosen for me. Now you must go and find yours."

Tsio wrapped his hand around hers, pressing it to his lips.

"I have already found it," he whispered into her palm. "My body is yours. My spirit is yours. And even if I am never united to you, the fires in my heart burn only for you. This way, you will always have a light to guide you home."

Akhila pulled her hand away, then flung her arms around Tsio's neck, pressing her cheek to his bare chest. The steady rhythm of his heart beat calmed her. She closed her eyes and drank in the warmth from his skin.

The last few months had been like a dream.

Akhila's return to the tribe had been cause for celebration. Neighboring communities had come from miles to give thanks to Raweno, for her safe return. A bountiful feast was presented, with endless cooking fires sending the smells of roasted game into the sky.

By night, Akhila regaled her people with the story of how she came to be joined with the body and soul of the salmon, how she met Poseidon, and eventually made her way home. The children in the tribe were all ears, hiding their faces behind hands with parted fingers, their eyes wide and mouths agape, never wavering from Akhila as she spoke.

"Akhila?" a tiny voice cried.

A small girl, no more than five stood beside her, drawing nervous doodles in the dirt with her bare toe. Akhila scooped up the child and placed her gently in her lap.

"What is it?" she asked.

"How did you keep from getting eaten by Onyare?"

Chuckles fluttered around the fire. Akhila smoothed the child's hair.

"I did not see the serpent of the great lakes," she replied. "For I went out into the deep ocean, Onyare does not live in the deep ocean."

The little girl smiled and wrapped her arms around Akhila's neck.

"I am so glad you are safe," she whispered.

Akhila gave the girl a squeeze.

"Me too, little sister," Akhila said. "But I am certain, if Onyare had been there, Poseidon and the salmon would have protected me."

The celebration lasted over a week. When the rejoicing and feasting finally died down, Akhila and the rest of her people got back to the business of living. The winter months had arrived, and Akhila relished in the gray skies, snowy trails and iced over streams that at one time had seemed like such a nuisance. Never had she felt such peace.

But there was an undertow. An unsettling and nervous feeling flowing through her. At first, Akhila tried to ignore it. But as the days turned into weeks, and then into months, the feelings of anxiousness could no longer be ignored. It came whenever she sat at the fire. Or, when she embraced her betrothed. But it was most ferocious when she slept. In her dreams she was swept up by a black current and dragged into deep caverns filled with fire. The dream came nightly. After two weeks, Akhila finally decided to take her problem to the tribal healer.

"Oka'ra?" she called out, poking her head in the doorway of the old shaman's longhouse.

Oka'ra Tkathos had built his home deep in the woods, nearly a day's walk from the rest of the Akwesasne. Secluded, he could submerse himself in every word the gods had to say and Oka'ra liked it that way.

"Are you looking for me?"

Akhila jumped and turned around. There knee deep in the snow, stood Oka'ra Tkathos, the seer of visions, staring back at her through the hollow eyes of his false face. Its red distorted features and long black flowing hair sent a shiver through her that rivaled even the coldest of winter days. Akhila shook off the nervousness and smiled.

"I am having dreams, Oka'ra," she said. "And they frighten me. Can you help?"

"Yes," he replied, pushing past her. As Oka'ra entered his longhouse, his voice echoed back. "Give me a moment. I have been expecting you."

Minutes crawled by as Akhila stood silent, shivering in the snow. Then Oka'ra stuck his head out the door and beckoned her inside.

Akhila stepped across the threshold of the shaman's longhouse, not sure what she expected to see. She had not been inside Oka'ra Tkathos's secluded home in many years. Most of her memories had faded, leaving behind only faint smells and blurry colors. As she looked around, Akhila found a modest dwelling, a warm fire and a comfortable place to sit.

"I hope I am not keeping you from some important work," Akhila said sitting down. "But I could think of no one else to go to about this problem."

Oka'ra smiled and handed her a small dream catcher. "My child, today, you *are* my important work."

Akhila gently fingered the small leather dream catcher, running the feathered tassels through the palm of her hand.

"Do you want me to hang this in the longhouse?" she asked.

Oka'ra shook his head. "No, we are going to try something unusual. I do not even know for sure that it will work. Hold the dream catcher out in front of you. As you tell me the dream, it's essence should become ensnared in the webs."

Akhila took a deep breath.

"It always starts the same," she began. "I am in the sea, then a woman with a tail like mine comes to me from the deep. I can never remember what she says to me, only that she wants me to follow her."

As the words flowed from her lips, the center of the dream catcher began to swirl and churn like a storm. The booming of thunder and crackling of lightening echoed from its core, a tiny self-contained cloudburst in the palms of her hands. Akhila stopped talking, mesmerized as raindrops and wind flooded from the dream catcher, misting her face.

"And do you?" Oka'ra asked.

Akhila nodded slowly, regaining her focus. "Yes. I hear many voices in the sea. They are singing a song I have never heard. Then the spirit of the ocean becomes angered and I am swept up by a ribbon of black water. I cannot fight against it and I cannot see through it. The current takes me to a river I have never been to before. Everything in it and around it is black and dead. The river leads to a cavern. I have to fight the urge to run away—"

"But you cannot?" Oka'ra interrupted.

"No," Akhila replied. "The river, the cavern, they cry out a name over and over."

"What name, do they call?" Oka'ra pressed.

"Orcus," Akhila whispered.

Akhila paused a moment and wiped the rain and sweat from her lip with the side of her arm.

"What of the fires?" Oka'ra said.

Akhila's eyes grew wide. "You know about the fires?"

"Yes," he replied. "From this side of the dream catcher, I can see into your dream. Tell me of the fires."

Akhila took a deep breath. "Once I enter the caverns, I can feel it growing warmer. As the opening of the cavern disappears behind me, I begin to see fire... wings of fire, scorching the cave walls. In some places, it's as if the walls themselves are made of fire."

Oka'ra reaches across and brushes a tear from her eye.

"Why do you grieve?" he whispers. "Tell me what else you see."

"There's a clearing," Akhila continues. "To the right there is sadness and longing. It is the place where unfulfilled spirits are forever in sorrow. To the right, there are two large doors. One is open, the other is closed and was once guarded by two, two headed beasts."

The storm in the dream catcher grew louder. Wind and rain gushed from the center, blowing back her hair. Akhila's hands began to struggle to hold on to the dream catcher.

"You must finish speaking the dream!" Oka'ra shouted over the storm.

Akhila pinched her eyes shut and continued to recount her dream into the catcher, while the thunder drowned out her voice. As the last word escaped her lips, the dream catcher jerked itself from her hands and landed in the fire.

Oka'ra instinctively lunged to intercept it, but the fire was faster. Within seconds, the tiny cloudburst was nothing more than smoke and steam.

"It is going to come true, isn't it?" Akhila asked.

The old shaman nodded. "Much of it, yes. You have been shown a turning point in your destiny."

Akhila stared at the floor. "I am frightened, Oka'ra. What if I refuse?"

Oka'ra stood up from the fire and walked out the door of the longhouse. As he disappeared into the whiteness of the snow, he called back to her.

"Destiny does not ask you, it tells you. Accept it

Akhila, or be overtaken by it. Those are your only choices."

That night there were no dreams. Her mind was static and blank, filled only with restless feelings and haunting voices, calling her back to the sea. Calling her to the dead river and the cavern of fire.

Akhila pulled away from Tsio's embrace.

"I have said my goodbyes to mother and father," she said. "Now I must say goodbye to you, Tsio."

Tsio nodded silently.

"It is my hope for you, that an honorable woman will give you many sons," she said, stepping into the frigid current of the river. As the water lapped up onto her skin, Akhila could feel her legs begin to fuse together, as the spirit of the river father began to take over her body. By the time she was waist deep in the Mohawk, her transformation was complete. Once again, Akhila was a mermaid.

"Akhila!" Tsio called out. "It is my hope that Hinon protects you in all your journeys."

She didn't respond with words. There was nothing more to say. Akhila dove head first into the river, her great silver tail breaching the water and splashing down behind her. As she sped down river towards the vast Atlantic Ocean, a raven leapt from its perch and began climbing into the gray January sky.

CHAPTER TWELVE

Heaven's Gate

The raven punched up through the clouds that served as the foundation Heaven's Gates were built on. As it came in for a landing, the raven's legs began to stretch. Its wings pulled back into its silky body, while slender arms began to emerge from its feathered sides. Within moments, the transformation was complete. The angel walked to the entrance of Heaven.

"Peter?" he sang out. "I have returned. Open the gate."

Simon Peter casually emerged from behind a tall, wooden pedestal, swinging a long gold chain attached to a key. With a single click, the gate was unlocked and swung inward, revealing the shimmering streets of Heaven.

"Are you staying with us long, Baracheil?" Peter asked. "Or will your duties take you from us once again?"

"There is much to do," the Archangel said, striding past the gate keeper. "I must see Nuriel, Sandalphon and Gabriel as soon as possible."

Simon Peter walked back to his pedestal and quickly began composing messages to the three Archangels.

"What should I tell them?"

"Tell them Atargatis will soon be delivering the mermaid to Hades," he replied over his shoulder. "We need to discuss the coming of the Orcus Child."

Chapter Thirteen

The Underworld

The first thing Malachi noticed was the smell. There was none. The air was silent, perfectly tempered and motionless. Glancing around, Malachi found no hellfire and damnation, no sulfuric blasts of smoke, and to his relief, no hounds of hell. Just ragged stone walls and a trail leading off into an archway of darkness, lit only by an occasional torch and decorated with marble statues of Greek gods. He pressed his hand against the wall. As it passed through, he breathed a sigh of relief.

"At least I know I can get back," he muttered.

"Perhaps. Perhaps not."

A strangely dressed figure stepped out from one of the many shadowed corners.

"One must be mindful of his surroundings at all times. Take nothing at face value and follow the rules, or you could be lost here forever."

Malachi raised a suspicious eyebrow. "You know this from experience?"

The stranger stepped fully into the light and gave a solemn nod.

"Some burdens can be learned from without being shared. I do not wish anyone to carry burdens like mine. So I am here to warn you... and guide you."

Malachi took a few steps towards the stranger to get a better look at his face. The stranger's face was battle warn, deep creases trenching a path alongside his nose down into the corners of his thin, tight mouth. Feathered lines fanned out from his almond shaped eyes, blending into a hairline filled with long black trusses, tightly tied at the top of his head. The gleam of sword's hilt peeked out from the folds of the sash around his waist.

"You are a warrior," Malachi said.

"Yes," the stranger replied. "I was once called Ruki Nagamatsu, a Samurai in the army of the first Shogun, Minamoto no Yoritomo. An arrow took my life during the battle of Ishibashiyama. My master went on to fight many battles. I came to rest here, in Yomi-no-kuni."

"I am grateful to be in the company of such a distinguished man," Malachi said with a smile. "My name is Malachi Ben Sinai,"

Ruki squared himself then bowed. "The honor is mine. It is not often that I am allowed to be in the presence of a general's son."

A deep sigh escaped Malachi's lungs.

"Did I say something to offend you?" Ruki asked.

"No, it is not anything you have said," Malachi grumbled, pressing his finger tips to his temples. "I just wish the title of 'General's Son' was hanging around the neck of someone else."

Ruki raised an eyebrow. "You are ashamed of being the son of Azazael?"

"I am ashamed of the curse he brought on himself and the attention it brings on me," Malachi answered.

The samurai lowered his gaze and shook his head.

"Do not despair," Malachi continued, "my father and I understand that our paths are different. He respects my choices and I accept his."

Ruki looked up at Malachi and gave him a nod.

"I understand. You are a most honored son, Malachi Ben Sinai. I am humbled and envious of your freedom."

Malachi blushed, his eyes darting around the space, looking for somewhere to escape the admiration radiating from Ruki's face. He wondered why immortals were always so in awe of him. Malachi grew weary of the special treatment bestowed on him because his father had been a rebel in Heaven.

"You are not dead," Ruki said, interrupting his thoughts.

"No," Malachi said, with a gruff. "I am very much alive."

"Why come into Yomi before your time?"

"I need to see a god about a soul," Malachi quipped.

"I uh—" Ruki replied, "I do not understand."

Malachi chuckled under his breath and shook his head. Balthazar would have appreciated the sarcasm.

"Forgive me, I need to see Orcus." Malachi said smiling. "Do you know where I can find him?"

Ruki nodded. "You mean Hades."

"I beg your pardon?" Malachi asked.

"You mean Hades." Ruki repeated. "That is his more common name. Very few call upon him by his Roman name anymore."

Malachi chuckled again. Of course Balthazar would have used the name Orcus. Most of his notes were written during their time in Rome.

"May I ask what you want with him?" Ruki continued.

"I am not sure," Malachi said, reaching for the pendant around his neck. "My closest friend needs my help. The only clue to his rescue was a note saying to come here."

"Strange that a living man would need help from the Of course, realm of the dead," Ruki said.

Malachi shook his head.

"If you knew the man, it would not seem strange at all," he said. "Lead the way."

Chapter Fourteen

The samurai and the sand dweller walked in silence. The occasional echoes of disembodied voices and the howling of unknown beasts were all that stood between them and the throne of Hades. Beyond that, the air remained still. Proving that death did truly hang within it. In the distance, beyond the sparse torch fire, was a much brighter glow. As the pair grew closer, Malachi could feel the atmosphere grow lighter and cooler, as if someone had thrown open a window and let in the breeze.

"We are close," Ruki said, breaking the long silence. "What you see and feel is the presence of Persephone. Even within the depths of death, she brings the spring."

They entered what appeared to be a throne room. At first glance, Malachi could make out the faint outlines of people standing idly on the wall near a pair of carved thrones.

"Interesting art design," Malachi whispered in Ruki's ear. "Is it supposed to be some strange play on Egyptian Hieroglyphs?"

"No," Ruki whispered back. "That is the royal court."

Malachi's attention drifted back to the outlines. Their motionless and expressionless presence was both unnerving and fascinating to him. He slowly walked across the throne room towards the mysterious figures, cocking his head from side to side, trying to find a crack in their facade.

"Malachi, please—" Ruki warned.

Malachi looked back at the samurai a moment.

"I just want to get a closer look,"

He continued to press forward until he was inches from the outlines on the wall. Resisting the urge to reach out and touch them, Malachi instead leaned in, staring down what appeared to be the expressionless face of a woman in front of him.

"You must stop," Ruki warned again. "I have to insist—"

Malachi glanced over his shoulder, a half grin inching up one side of his face.

"Why?" he asked. "What is a painting on a wall going to do?"

Ruki put his hands up.

Malachi turned his attention back to the wall, peering into the woman's face. She was a beautiful depiction of a typical Greek aristocrat.

"Who were you in life, my Lady?" he asked gently.

The woman's vacant stare shifted in their sockets, fixing their gaze on Malachi's face. The long and regal curls that cascaded down her back, began to flutter like a sail in the wind. The woman's brow, once soft and passive pulled into a deep frown as her pouty mouth opened to reveal rows of jagged, rotted teeth. She let out a roar, then lunged from the wall, knocking Malachi flat on his back.

He wriggled and squirmed under the woman, but she gripped his wrists like iron cuffs and the weight of her body crushed his chest like the anchor of a ship. It took only seconds for him to concede.

"Release me!" he hollered. "I apologize... please!"

The woman continued to snarl and growl, snapping at his face like a rabid dog.

Malachi turned away, trying to avoid the smell and the drool coming from the rotted out remains of the woman's mouth.

"That will do, Eudokia. The young man seems to have received your message loud and clear."

The woman looked up and growled. Then slowly backed away on all fours, back towards the wall. Malachi sat up and watched, as Eudokia rose to her feet, then blended back into the stone, once again becoming nothing more than a figure in a mural.

"I hope she didn't harm you... much."

Malachi looked behind him and saw the god of the Greek underworld, Hades standing behind him.

"No, she did not," Malachi said, "but I will admit, for a moment I was unsure of my fate."

Hades shrugged his shoulders then began to walk towards the pair of carved thrones.

"Pity," he said. "I was ready to see some blood. Oh well, no matter,"

Malachi rose to his feet. As he started to step towards the throne, a hand shot out, grabbing him by Of course, the arm. He turned and saw Ruki standing beside him, one hand around Malachi's forearm, the other on the handle of his blade. Malachi stared at him, his brows pulled down over his eyes like the eaves of a house.

"Take your hands off me," Malachi said through clenched teeth. "He does not even know my business here, and yet he insults me!"

Ruki dug his fingers in to Malachi's arm. "Do not invoke the wrath of Hades," he warned. "You are in his world. He will not tolerate insolence—"

"Insolence!?" Malachi bellowed.

"Shhh..." Ruki hissed.

Malachi lowered his voice to a near whisper and continued. "Insolence? I have come to him for help, I am almost killed by some devil woman painted on a wall, and yet I must keep *my* insolence in check?"

"You do know I can hear everything the two of you are saying?" Hades sighed. "Come forward, both of you."

Like scolded children, Malachi and Ruki walked to the center of the throne room and faced Hades. There they stood in silence, while Hades nonchalantly primped his dark, flowing robes, pleating the layers with his fingers and smoothing out the long, tattered sleeves. He dragged the preening out for several minutes, humming under his breath, all the while keeping one eye on the two warriors standing impatiently before him. Finally, the god of the Greek underworld rested his arms at his sides and settled back in his throne.

"Now," he continued, "let us begin again. Come, sit beside me Malachi, and tell me why you would travel all the way into Hades just to talk to me."

Malachi turned and faced Ruki.

"I will be right here," Ruki said. "It is not often one gets the privilege of addressing Hades so informally. Go."

Malachi walked up the steps to the pair of thrones, then gazed hesitantly at the throne of Persephone.

"What of the queen?" he asked.

Hades smiled. "She is near. Please, sit."

Malachi planted himself in the vacant seat next to Hades. His eyes darted around the expanse of the throne room, taking in with awe, what Hades took for granted. Every wall was adorned with iron torches as large as a man, every corner filled with ornately painted clay pots of every size. The floor was covered with intricately detailed mosaics, in different shades of black and gray stones all framed in long flowing dark blue silk sheers that hung from somewhere in the blackness of the ceiling. The delicate cloth casually drifted in some unknown breeze that seemed to creep through the space like a specter.

His eyes fell on the wall containing Hades's 'court'. Malachi let out a deep breath and shook his head.

"They were once the talk of Greece, every one of them," Hades said, motioning towards the painting. "Aristocrats, land owners, the most rich and powerful and *beautiful* of the Greek islands. Every one of them would have spit on their own mothers to get ahead in the world. And so, when they died—"

"You repaid the favor?"

Hades grinned. "Yes. In death, they will spend their days acknowledging my greatness, the way they insisted on being undeservedly acknowledged during their insignificant lives. I despise mortal ego."

He shifted in his seat. Facing Malachi, Hades leaned on his elbow, then gave his guest an upward nod.

"You are no mortal," he said with gentle voice. "What could you possibly need from he who rules over mortal death?"

Malachi reached back and untied the leather cord

attached to the defixio he wore around his neck. He held it in his hand a moment. It had been hundreds of years since Malachi first promised to safeguard the curse tablet containing Balthazar's soul, and the first time since that day he had ever taken it off. He pictured Balthazar on the stake in Scotland, burning. Burning because of him. Burning while he himself could do nothing but stand in the crowd and watch. Malachi brushed off the memory and held the necklace out to Hades.

"Do you know what this is?" he asked.

Hades took the defixio from Malachi. "Yes I do. They were very popular in ancient Rome. Is that when you acquired it?"

"Yes," Malachi answered. "Or rather, that is when my friend and I commissioned it."

The god of the underworld turned the rolled piece of lead over in his hands, stroking his thumb over the smooth head of the gold nail that ran through its center. Then he held it up to his ear, as if it were a conch discovered on the shore. Hades listened for a minute, his eyes growing wide.

"I see," he said. "You make a very valid point."

Malachi sat staring at Hades, his mouth agape. "Can you—"

Hades held his hand up, continuing to listen intently to the message coming from the curse tablet.

"Yes," he replied. "I will relay your message, Balthazar."

As Malachi sat stunned on the throne of Persephone, Hades gingerly placed the defixio back in his hand.

"Y-you c-an talk—"

"Of course," Hades said. "But first things first."

Hades reached beside his throne and yanked on a heavy, braided cord. A moment later, two men, dressed in nothing more than leather loin cloths skittishly entered the throne room, heads down.

"These men are guests of the palace," Hades bellowed. "See that they have accommodations and have the banquet hall set up for a feast this evening."

The two slaves nodded without a word then backed out of the room in haste. Malachi eyed Hades suspiciously.

"So, Ruki and I are to remain here, then?"

Hades nodded. "The journey your friend is about to send you on is going to be perilous to your heart. But do not fear, Balthazar has a plan."

CHAPTER FIFTEEN

An hour later Hades, Malachi and Ruki sat at a long banquet table, while scores of silent slaves bustled around the room pouring wine and setting out lavish trays of fresh produce, breads and fish.

Hades snatched a bunch of bulging, blood red grapes and began popping them into his mouth one at a time.

"These are vintage grapes," Hades said, smacking his lips. "Left as an offering to me in a temple over a thousand years ago. They are just as delicious now, as they were when I first received them."

"How is that possible?" Malachi scoffed, studying the bowl with disbelieve.

Ruki smiled and drained his glass. "You see Malachi, time has its own set of rules in the underworld,"

Malachi reached out and plucked a grape from the bowl.

"It is perfectly safe," Ruki continued. "In the living world, many years have passed, but here, it has been only moments."

He took a deep breath, then ate the grape. As Malachi's teeth pressed down on the ancient fruit, a burst of perfectly sweetened juice flooded his mouth.

"My word!" he exclaimed.

"I told you," Ruki said.

"As delicious now, as the day they were dedicated,"

Hades sighed, raising his goblet.

Relieved, Malachi reached across the table for a loaf of bread. As his hand began to close around the crusty loaf, Ruki's palm shot out and slapped it away. The bread sailed down the table and landed with a thump on the tile floor.

"What the..." Malachi said, "Why did you do that?"

"I cannot allow you to eat anything prepared."

"What are you talking about?" Malachi asked, glancing over at Hades. "What is he talking about?"

Hades shrugged, a mischievous glimmer peeking out of the corner of his eye.

"Food that is pure and unchanged will do you no harm," Ruki warned, "but never eat anything that has been prepared in a hearth of the underworld. Once the food is changed, it will change you."

"What would happen to me?" Malachi asked.

"You would become a permanent resident," Hades mumbled.

Malachi abruptly shoved his chair back and stood up.

"You were going to let me eat it!" he shouted, pointing an accusing finger in Hades's face.

Hades shrugged his shoulders again, smiling.

"I cannot be responsible for every above ground tourist who dares to venture unprepared into my world," Hades snickered. "Buyer beware, young Sand Dweller,"

"This is preposterous!"

"Oh sit down!" Hades replied. "Preposterous indeed! You have been spending too much time with Englishmen, Malachi, you are starting to sound like an entitled, pompous, old snob."

Malachi and Hades stared at each other a few moments, jaws locked, eyes boring into one another. Malachi thought about the months he had spent with Reginald. The rules. The pomp and circumstance and all the endless fanfare that went with every little piece of English life. As memories fluttered past his eyes, Malachi began to smile. Then he began to chuckle. Soon, Ruki and Hades joined in and before long, the roar of their laughter filled the corridors of Hades's palace. Malachi wiped away a tear from his laughter ridden face and sat back down.

Malachi sat back down in his seat. "Forgive me," he said, grabbing another grape.

Hades's shoulders bobbed up and down as his own laughter began to subside.

"All is forgiven, my dear guest," he said, "I have not had a good belly laugh like that in many years. Any debt you owe me has been paid."

"Well," Ruki said, "I think it is time we discuss more important matters."

Hades wiped his mouth. "Yes, you are absolutely right. Malachi, Balthazar has a plan to free himself from the curse tablet."

Malachi leaned forward, his mouth agape.

"The Fates can remove his soul from the defixio, but only if there is a new vessel to put it in. That is where you come in."

"Me?" Malachi quizzed. "What can I do?"

Hades cleared his throat.

"I uh, understand you have a lady friend residing in the Ninth Circle?"

Malachi closed his eyes.

"A young half demon named, Zilpah?" Hades pressed, leaning forward.

"What about her?" Malachi asked through clenched teeth.

"A coupling with her, within the walls of the underworld, will produce a soulless child," Hades replied. "The Fates can use that child as the vessel for Balthazar's soul."

Malachi shook his head. "No."

"It is the only way."

"I cannot," Malachi repeated.

"You must!" Hades yelled, slamming his fist onto the table. "If you truly wish to help your friend, you will use your hatred for that creature to your advantage."

"Hades is right," Ruki said, placing his hand on Malachi's shoulder. "It truly is the only way."

Malachi stood back up and began to pace back and forth along the length of the table. To lie with Zilpah would be like crawling into a lion's den. He ran his hands through his hair, thinking of their last meeting. Her hands, warm and soft, running along the length of his bare leg. The scent of that musky perfume that followed her through the centuries. The evil she inflicted on his closest friend in order to have him all to herself.

"I do not know if I can—"

Hades smiled and leaned back in his chair.

"Do not fear," he said, "she will no doubt bewitch your body into submission. She will think she is trapping you, when in reality, she will be doing all the work for you. All you have to do is lie back and let it happen. Then, in nine months time—"

"Nine months?" Malachi yelled. "Do you expect me to wait around here for nearly a year?"

"It will go by faster than you realize," Ruki chimed in. "Remember, time has its own set of rules in the realm of the dead."

"And you actually believe his plan will work?" Malachi asked.

"Oh yes," Hades replied, stroking his bottom lip with the tip of his finger. "I know it will work."

Another group of servants entered the banquet hall, some carrying trays of pomegranates and more wine, while others came to clear away empties. As they passed by him, Malachi couldn't believe his eyes. Her skin was faded and gray, except for a small pair of puncture marks on her neck that glowed red and swollen. The servant looked at Malachi for just a second, before pardoning herself in Italian and setting the tray she was carrying on the table.

"Lucette?" Malachi cried, grabbing the servant by the arms.

The girl stared blankly into his face.

"Lucette!" Malachi yelled, shaking her, "Lucette it is me! Mio caro, it is Malachi."

His panic-stricken face darted around the room.

"Why will she not answer me?"

"She cannot," Ruki said. "When she died, she left her memories behind."

Malachi gently took her chin in his hand and turned her face to one side, exposing the marks on her neck. Anxiety flooded his stomach. Zilpah had done this. She had once again taken someone away from him. Lucette's glazed and vacant eyes told him all he needed to know. Zilpah would never stop. She would follow him into every century and destroy everyone he dared care about.

Malachi leaned in and gently kissed her cheek, then released his grip on Lucette. The servant girl immediately grabbed up the empty trays from the table and carried them out of the banquet hall. With his back to Hades and Ruki, he nodded slowly.

"Very well," Malachi conceded, "I will do it. How do we get Zilpah here?"

"I dispatched a messenger with a note into Hell before we sat down to dine." Hades said. "She will no doubt intercept it. All we need to do is set the trap, and wait."

Chapter Sixteen

The Atlantic Ocean, September, 1592

Atargatis clung tightly to the torso of the bull shark, careful to keep herself hidden behind the beast's girth. Her own shimmering tail, its fins feathering out into the sea, kept in sync with the steady back and forth sway of the sharks own muscular fin. She ran her clawed hand up and down the length of the shark's belly, while she lovingly pressed her cheek to its chest.

"That's right," Atargatis purred, stroking the bull shark, "just a little further and then we shall make our move."

She peered out from under the shark at her prize. In the distance, swam a young mermaid, who seemed completely unaware that she was being stalked. Atargatis licked her lips as the shark inched closer. The timing had to be just right. Her Siren sisters required a perfect sacrifice, and with the Turning of the Tide only a few weeks away, Atargatis couldn't afford to lose such a lovely offering.

The young mermaid continued her course, meandering through the open ocean, occasionally diving down into the blackness, then shooting up and through the surface of the water. With flawless form, she would reenter the sea, hardly leaving a splash or a ripple.

Atargatis stifled her envious heart. It had been too many centuries since she herself had felt that free spirited. So much time had passed since her transformation, she feared one day her former life would cease to have ever been. She shrugged off the worries. Now was not the time to wallow in pity. Atargatis gave her companion another stroke on his belly.

"Now, my pet," she growled, "go and fetch my prize!"

She released her grip on the bull shark.

The beast shot through the water. It took only seconds for the shark to close the distance between him and the unsuspecting mermaid. Like a jack hammer, the bull shark rammed his nose into the mermaid's back. The force of the blow pushed the air from her lungs, sending a cloud of bubbles into the sea. Then his jaws widened, displaying several rows of razor-sharp teeth. As the shark turned to make another pass, Atargatis swam out and positioned herself between the lifeless mermaid and the shark.

"No!" she commanded, raising her palm to the beast. "She is mine."

The shark barreled down on Atargatis, its mouth agape.

As the beast closed in, Atargatis squared herself, arms wide. When the shark's snout was in arms reach, Atargatis swiped her clawed hand across his face. Deep gashes opened up like a fan, destroying his left eye and clouding the water with blood.

Disoriented, the bull shark began to thrash.

"You dare to defy me?" Atargatis raged, taking another deadly swipe at the shark. "You who is nothing more than a mindless beast of burden?"

In her fury, Atargatis continued to rip and claw at the shark, until the beast stopped moving. Panting, she pulled back and surveyed the damage. What was once a terror of the ocean, the shark had been reduced to little more than a floating piece of flesh. Atargatis reached out and ripped away a chunk of meat from the shark's back. Then she raised it to her lips and casually took a bite. The sweet and fishy flesh melted in her mouth. Atargatis inhaled deeply, filling the gills behind her ears with salt water and the dead shark's blood.

"What happened?"

Atargatis spun around.

The young mermaid cautiously approached, her hands pressed against either side of her lower back.

"I was about to dive, when something hit me from behind," the mermaid said.

Atargatis swallowed her mouthful of shark and smiled.

"Yes, my dear," she said, "you were rammed by a shark. It intended to eat you, but I killed it before it could."

The mermaid's eyes fell on the remains of the bull shark. She shuttered and looked away.

"Oh how horrible," she said. "The predatory creatures have never tried to harm me before. I am indebted to you for your kindness."

"There there now, my child," Atargatis sighed, reaching out a hand. "You would surely have done the same for me. My name is Atargatis. Some have called me the goddess of fertility and the sea. What should I call you?"

"I am Akhila, Mermaid of the Flint Place," the young

mermaid replied.

Atargatis nodded.

"Well, Akhila, I was on my way to the islands of Leukai, for the Turning of the Tide. It is only a seven days journey. Would you like to accompany me?"

"Leukai?" Akhila asked.

"Do not tell me you know not of the Sirens of Leukai, or the Turning of the Tide ceremony?" Atargatis said. "You are a mermaid, are you not?"

Akhila shrugged her shoulders, a flush of crimson embarrassment washing over her cheeks.

"I have only been in this form about a year," Akhila admitted. "There is still much about the sea I have yet to learn."

Atargatis glided around Akhila, swirling her tail through the water like silk on a breeze. *This child is a naive little creature,* she thought. She stopped behind the young mermaid, hovering once more in the water.

"The Turning of the Tide does not begin for more than a fortnight," she said, placing her hands gently on Akhila's shoulders. "As we travel to the warm waters of the Mediterranean, I could teach you our ways. How would that be?"

"Really?" Akhila beamed. "You would do that for me?"

A smile raised the corners of Atargatis's mouth. She leaned in close, her lips brushing against the young mermaid's ear.

"Have you ever felt a pull within yourself, an urge, to do *something,* but you knew not what it was that you should do?"

"Yes," Akhila nodded, her mouth agape. "How did you know?"

"There is much magic inside of you, Akhila of the Flint Place," Atargatis said. "Those urges you feel, is your magical self trying to come out. I will teach you how."

Atargatis released Akhila's shoulders.

As Akhila turned and faced her, the Syrian goddess reached out her hand.

"Come with me," she prodded.

Akhila smiled and took her hand.

CHAPTER SEVENTEEN

Heaven

Sandalphon neatly folded his wings against his back and strode into the hall, sea water still dripping off the tips of his shoulder length hair.

"Would you like something to dry off with?"

A young man walked past him, hauling an armload of scrolls. He dropped the pile on a small desk in the corner, then opened the top drawer and pulled out a neatly folded towel. Then on silent feet, he padded over to the water-logged angel.

"Here, use this," the young man said, handing Sandalphon the towel. "I cannot have you dripping all over my nice, clean floor."

Sandalphon shook open the towel and draped it over his head.

"Thank you, Aaron," the angel said. "Please send my deepest apologies to the tile."

Aaron smiled and stuck his tongue out.

The archangel wandered the hall, observing the walls lined with shelves, jam packed with scrolls, some dating back to the very beginning. There were great record halls like this one all over Heaven, some housing human histories, some housing life and death records. Halls for fiction written by humans as well as halls to house music and art. But Sandalphon loved this one the most. It was the Hall of Hopes, where Heaven stored all the hopes and dreams of the future, where every desire that glorified the Most High was housed until needed.

Its curator was a wise angel named Aaron. In spite of being a low level member of the Heavenly Host, Aaron was held with great esteem. His knowledge of the future was rivaled by none, save the Most High, Himself. He lovingly and methodically protected and preserved man's hopes and dreams as if they were his own.

Sandalphon was constantly inspired by him.

"Am I the first to arrive again?"

Aaron's eyes peeked over the top of the pile of scrolls on his desk.

"You are always the first to arrive."

The archangel nodded and continued to wander along the perimeter, taking stock of the bulging shelves.

Aaron watched from behind the scrolls a moment. He smiled as Sandalphon moved on to the next tower of shelves.

"Stop," he called out. "Want to read one I just received?"

Sandalphon turned, a joyous smile spreading across his face.

"Can I?" he asked.

"Third shelf, second from the end on the right," Aaron replied, "It was sent to me by mistake. It should be stored over in languages. You will get a kick out of it."

Sandalphon reached up and pulled down the scroll. On the left handle of the scroll was a single word: CONTRACTIONS.

"What is this, Aaron?" Sandalphon said, unrolling the parchment.

"It is the combining of two words together in order to make one word," Aaron said. "Languages has been sending down scrolls like that one periodically for about six hundred years. That one is not scheduled to go down for another four centuries."

"Wouldn't, isn't, can't, I'd," Sandalphon recited. "These are great!"

"Yes well," Aaron said, shaking his head, "they appeal to the eternal impatience of man. They are always in such a hurry, even when they talk. You should read some of the scrolls that are scheduled to go down in the twenty first century. The hall of languages has a scroll that will condense whole sentences in to just a few letters."

Sandalphon chuckled under his breath and placed the scroll back on the shelf.

"Are we late?" a voice echoed from the entrance.

Sandalphon looked up and smiled as Baracheil, Nuriel and Gabriel entered the Hall of Hopes. His heart swelled with love for his angelic brothers. They had fought many battles together in the early days. After the fall of Lucifer, the remaining Archangels had been handed down new tasks, all meant to protect and strengthen the fledgling human race. Those tasks kept the angels too busy to interact most of the time. So he welcomed this special assignment. The old team, together again.

"Why is the floor wet?" Nuriel asked, tip-toeing over a small puddle.

Laughter rang out in the hall as the four archangels sat down at the long, heavy table that rested in the center.

Sandalphon reached up and pulled the now damp towel off his head.

"While the rest of you have been enjoying fair weather, I was beneath a thousand fathoms of the cold Atlantic sea."

Aaron silently walked around the table, setting down goblets of ambrosia. Then he absently reached down and retrieved the wet towel from the floor and tucked it under his arm.

"Play nice boys," he mumbled under his breath.

Gabriel shook his head then took a large pull from his goblet.

"How did it go?" he asked, wiping his lips on the back of his hand. "Did you have any trouble with Atargatis?"

"No," Sandalphon replied. "She never knew I was there."

Nuriel raised an eyebrow. "Really, how? Did you disguise yourself as a fish this time?"

"I became a part of the ocean," Sandalphon said. "I had not done an elemental change in quite some time."

Laughter erupted around the table.

"What?" he continued. "I need the practice!"

Gabriel stood and walked over to where Sandalphon was sitting. Then he gave the archangel a hearty clap on the back.

"My brother, you are a perfectionist,"

"I cannot help it," Sandalphon sighed, "I love them too much. I am the guardian over all the guardians. Being a silent protector is my business."

"Well said," Baracheil chimed in. "Let us move on to phase two. Gabriel, what of our petition to enter Hell?

Will the Most High allow it?"

"The outer realms of the underworld, yes, but we are forbidden from entering Lucifer's domain."

"How are we to retrieve the Orcus child, if we cannot enter the dark gates?" Nuriel asked.

Gabriel shook his head. "I have not figured that out yet."

"I have," Sandalphon said.

All eyes turned to him.

"The whole point of this mission is to retrieve the child without being seen," Sandalphon began. "That was the whole reason for using the mermaid in the first place, right?"

"Yes but," Baracheil said.

"But nothing," Sandalphon continued. "She will take the child because she is a mermaid and it is in her nature. Because she is also a human, she will take the child to her people."

Baracheil shrugged his shoulders. "So?"

"As a guardian, I know a little something about people," Sandalphon replied. "And her people are Iroquois. They will trust us, in fact, I believe they will give the child to us willingly."

Nuriel leaned in. "What makes you so sure?"

"Because they are already familiar with angels," Sandalphon quipped. "We are known as 'The Thunders,' amongst The People of the Flint Place."

Chapter Eighteen

The Underworld

Malachi stepped across the threshold of his lodgings. The grapes in his belly had blended with his nerves to form a heavy lump that rested in his guts like an omen. As he sat on the edge of the massive bed in the center of the room, Malachi contemplated the things to come. Part of him couldn't deny the attraction he had for Zilpah. With or without her bewitchings, there were moments he longed to lay with her. Perhaps it was that musky scent that had followed her through the centuries since the days of Josiah and the palace in Judah. His mind wandered back to the first time he saw her. That raven hair and the impish look behind her eyes. Suddenly her face faded from his memory. There in her place stood the pale remains of Lucette, with a pair of holes in her neck and tears streaking her cheeks.

"Damn it all!" he cried out, standing up.

He lifted his arms over his head and stretched. Would she come tonight? Tomorrow? His mind and body seemed to be deadlocked.

Ruki poked his head in through the doorway that connected their rooms. In his hands were a pair of gold chalices and a jug of wine.

"Are you well?" he whispered. "I heard you shouting."

Malachi dropped his arms to his sides and began to pace the room.

"Yes, I am well."

"Take care," Ruki warned, stepping into the room. "Always be aware of the things you say out loud here. You never know who will be listening."

Malachi ran his hands through his hair and sat back down on the bed.

"I think that rule applies no matter where you are, my friend. I am sorry if I disturbed you."

"Not at all," Ruki replied, sitting down in an overstuffed chair. "I do not sleep."

"I do not do much sleeping myself," Malachi said.

The samurai sat the drink and cups down on a small table, then leaned forward, resting his elbows on his knees.

"Tell me," Ruki said, "about your friend, Balthazar. Why have you gone to such lengths for this man?"

"When Balthazar learned of my lineage," Malachi began, "he took it upon himself to help me. Got me out of Jerusalem before I could be discovered. Bartered passage to Rome and helped me start a new life. All the while, searching for a way to break the curse handed down to me from my father."

Ruki stroked his chin. "He sounds like a trusted companion."

"Oh he is and so much more," Malachi continued. "When he had exhausted all human resources, he—"

The samurai leaned forward. "What did he do?"

"He paid a priestess to conjure a demon, to have an immortal curse put on himself so he would have all the time he needed to find a cure for mine."

Malachi leaned back on the bed. The rocky ceiling above him was covered with detailed paintings of ancient Greek life. His eyes zeroed in on a small scene where it depicted a man who had fallen into the mouth of a hole filled with fire, his two-dimensional hand outstretched to another who was desperately trying to help him escape death.

"Balthazar risked everything, even his eternity for my sake," Malachi said. "His sacrifice will not be for nothing."

Ruki nodded.

"It will not be in vain," he said. "The best of us will give up everything that is ours to give, in order that our brothers may be better off than they were before. Even if there is nothing given in return."

"You believe that?" Malachi asked.

Ruki stood up and walked to the door leading to his bed chambers. He stopped short of entering his room, turned and glanced at Malachi over his shoulder.

"You do not?"

"I hope I can do this thing that Hades wants me to do," Malachi mumbled.

"Ah, you mean lay with the demon woman?" Ruki asked.

Malachi nodded.

Ruki threw his head back and let out a hearty belly laugh.

"Never have I seen a man so worried about something that should come natural to him," he chuckled. "I would say have some of the wine, but you cannot. That reminds me—"

Ruki started back across the room to retrieve the jug.

As he reached for the cups, Malachi grabbed his hand.

"No," he said. "Leave it."

The samurai eyed him curiously.

"Why?"

"Because after this is all over, I intend to leave the underworld with Balthazar," Malachi said. "And I do not wish to be followed."

CHAPTER NINETEEN

The Gates of Hell

The servant's hands shook as he lifted the folded piece of parchment to the nose of the hell-hound. With a suspicious eye, the beast looked over the document. Fire flicked and danced in the many open wounds that covered its body, a grim reminder that even Lucifer's favorite pets were made from the very essence of Hell itself. The beast inhaled deeply, taking in all the words imbedded in the pages. With a gruff, the hell-hound blasted a cloud of sulfur from its nostrils, then stood aside.

With careful steps, the servant pulled open the rusted, iron gate that led to the deepest level of the underworld. The crusted hinges cried out in protest, its screams echoing through the blackened tunnel that lay beyond. As he stepped through the opening, the servant noticed the temperature instantly rise, and even without his body, which was safe and sound in the family tomb, he could feel the prickles where sweat would have pushed out onto his skin.

As he inched forward, the hell-hound let out an ear-piercing howl, then whipped his tail, slamming the gate shut. The screech of metal on metal made him jump, but the servant quickly regained his composure. After walking a few yards, sconces filled with flames began to appear on the walls. Then passages that let to other parts of Hell opened up all around him.

The servant kept his senses alert, remembering what his master had told him:

"Wander the halls of Lucifer's domain until you find the half-demon called Zilpah. When you find her, tell her you have a message from Malachi to his father. She must be made to believe she has intercepted the correspondence."

The instructions were simple enough.

He pushed on, focusing on the task at hand. The deeper the servant descended, the louder Hell became. Moans and wails from tortured souls bounced off the stone walls, the weight of their despair so heavy, they blew on the sconce flames like wind. The occasional soul, quivering and emaciated, would pass in the darkness. Never making eye contact, the souls of the damned clung to the walls and held their phantom breath in eternal fear.

The corridor stretched for what seemed like miles, lined with heavy, stone doors. His eyes stole quick glances as he passed the opened ones, and was filled with horrors each time.

Finally, he came upon a door, carved from stone and looming like a mountain. As he approached it, the servant found it ajar. Inside, with his back to the door, was a giant of a demon, naked from the waist down. Before him, knelt a young girl with hollow caverns for eyes, greedily suckling on his phallus, while her webbed hands kneaded his sack. Off to the side, amidst a deep pile of cushions and wraps, lay the half demon, Zilpah. Though her hands were hidden beneath layers of black silk, her moans gave away their dirty secret.

The servant's eyes widened, as Zilpah cried out, her orgasm rumbling through him like an earthquake. Smiling, she opened her eyes and stared at him with lust. With one hand, she reached out beckoning the servant in, while the other stroked her already hardened nipples.

As he entered the room, the servant pulled the parchment from his tunic.

"Pardon me," he stuttered, holding out the letter. "I am looking for General Azazael. This letter is to be delivered to him from his son, Malachi."

Zilpah bolted upright.

"I see," she said, straightening her skirts.

"If you could just direct me to his quarters," the servant started.

Zilpah shook her head and took a step towards him.

"Nonsense," she cooed. "One could get lost if one does not know his way. Let me take it for you. I promise it will be delivered safely."

The servant's hand shook, hesitantly.

"I know the General personally," she pressed with a Cheshire cat grin.

A roar filled the chamber as the demon finally achieved his orgasm.

Zilpah glanced over her shoulder at the demon and smiled.

"Come on," she whispered. "Give me the note. Ba'al is always hungry after he has had one of his domestics. We would not want you to become his next meal."

With a shiver, the servant handed over the parchment. He then offered a clumsy bow.

"T-thank you," he stuttered, backing out of the room. "I will just take my leave now."

As the servant left Ba'al's chambers, Zilpah shook her head. Nervous little servants from the underworld were most entertaining. Most of them, having no knowledge of the Ninth Circle itself, were horrified at the abounding atrocities that made up daily life in The Ninth Circle. She turned on her heel and returned to her pile of cushions. Flopping down, Zilpah ran her sharpened fingernail under the wax seal of Hades and popped it off, flinging the smoky black wax to the floor. She watched the heat of Hell's fire radiate through the stone floor, causing the wax to burst in to flame. Within moments, the seal was nothing more than a smoldering pile of ash. Then she sat back, opened up the letter and began to read:

Father,

Circumstances have brought me to the realm of Hades for a brief stay. I was unable to bring
my human chaperone, so I find myself quite alone in an environment unfamiliar to me. My
dealings with Hades will keep me here for a very short time and I could certainly use someone
such as yourself to aide me in my negotiations. I do not wish to elaborate, but would rather
discuss my dealings with you in person.

Your Son,
Malachi

Zilpah dropped the letter on the floor, its edges catching fire instantly.

"Well, well, well," she whispered, "my delicious conquest has finally arrived."

She reached behind her and grabbed hold of a large whip hanging on the wall. Then she gave it a crack, sending its long, fiery strap out into the room, the studded tip connecting with the bare back of Ba'al's sex servant.

"Gather my best silks, my oils and send for someone to attend to my hair," Zilpah barked at the soul. "I will be departing Hell in a few hours."

***

The servant slipped back through the gate, relieved to be heading back to the even-tempered atmosphere of Hades. The hell-hound snarled at the servant's back, once again slamming shut the gate with its leathery tail.

"Is it done?"

The servant dropped to one knee in reverence.

"Yes, my lord, she suspected nothing." he replied.

The god of the underworld nodded in approval.

"You have done well," he said. "You may return to your duties."

As the soul slipped away quietly, a cool breeze picked up Hade's robes. Then a delicate hand ran along his back, stopping at his neck, before continuing up into his hair.

"You know, I do this all for you," he whispered.

Persephone slipped her free arm around his waist.

"I know, my love."

CHAPTER TWENTY

andles lit the corners of the room, casting wavy shadows across the walls. At Malachi's request, two servants had brought in vases filled with lavender sprigs and honeysuckle vines. Soon their soft aroma drifted throughout the space, creating a veil that separated Malachi's bed chamber from the rest of the underworld.

He stripped off his clothes and threw them casually in the chair vacated by Ruki only a few hours earlier. For a few moments he just stood in the center of the room, letting the scent of the flowers and the warmth coming off the candles wash over his bare skin. As his eyes wandered, they fell on a large carved mirror tucked away in one of the corners. It had been a long time since he had looked upon his naked body. Malachi let out a deep sigh and turned away. This was no time for gawking.

He pulled back the satin bedclothes and climbed in, the cool fabric sending electric shivers up his legs. Then he leaned his head back on the cushions, tucked one arm under his head and let the other drape lazily down the side of the bed. As the silence of the room took over, Malachi could hear the steady rhythm of his heart own beat, filling his head with steady hypnotic pulses. It was like the drums of Egypt that had called him to Judah all those years ago. Where he had stood before King Josiah, where he had pledged his very life to the king. Where he had first laid eyes on Zilpah. Like a built-in lullaby, the beats were calming. His breath grew slower. Malachi sunk himself deeper into the pile of pillows and drifted off to sleep.

***

Zilpah stood just beyond the light of the candles for what seemed like hours, watching him sleep. With her head cocked to one side, she looked on, fascinated and overwhelmed by his body. Lean, and deeply bronzed, Malachi was beautiful. She silently padded across the floor on bare feet, then standing beside the bed, Zilpah reached out and gently caressed his bare chest with the back of her hand, while her eyes never wavered from his face. As her hand glided down, Zilpah found Malachi's warm flesh replaced by the coolness of the satin wrapped around his hips. With a slow squeeze, she grasped a handful of his thigh, the tightness of his muscles causing a gasp to escape her throat.

Malachi shifted in his bed. His closed eyes fluttered a moment, then he sighed.

"Zilpah," he muttered.

A smile spread across her face.

"So," she whispered, releasing her grip on his thigh, "he dreams of me."

She walked around to the other side of the bed and climbed in. Then gently she lifted her silken skirts and straddled Malachi.

"Wake up, Malachi," she whispered, raking her fingers down his chest. "Open your eyes."

Malachi stirred, then came to.

"Wha..." he mumbled, reaching for her hands. "Zilpah? What are you doing here?"

"Shhh," she hissed, "I heard you call out to me in your sleep. Do not fight me. This night has been beckoning to us for a long time."

Malachi released his grip on her, then ran his hands through his hair.

"You should not be here, Zilpah," he began.

"Oh yes I should," she replied. "Since the moment you first discovered me behind that pillar in Josiah's palace, you *knew* you were destined to be mine. Just as I am yours. Do not make me enchant you, Malachi. It will be so much sweeter, if you would take me of your own free will."

Zilpah steadied herself on her knees, then reached up and took hold of her silk wraps. Slowly, she pulled them down to her waist, baring her full breasts to him.

"Please," she begged with a breathless whisper. "I am yours for the taking."

The weight of his lust hit Malachi square in the chest. He sat up, taking her firm buttocks in his hands and burying his face in her breasts. Returning the sentiment, Zilpah plunged her fingers in to his hair and pulled him close, relishing in the arousal.

"Oh yes," she moaned, "I want to feel you inside me."

Malachi released her swollen nipple from between his teeth, then rolled her over onto her back. He reached down and yanked off her silk wraps and flung them to the floor. He hovered over her a moment, drinking in the curves of her body.

"You are so beautiful Zilpah," he said, "but I feel I may live to regret this night."

Zilpah leaned back into the pillows and opened her legs.

"No regrets," she cooed, "just two creatures of the dark, coming together to create their own light."

His manhood hard and ready, Malachi thrust his hips forward and pushed himself into her. Another moan escaped her lips as he pumped in and out, the wetness of her sex coating him with desire. He pulled her lips close to his and kissed her, his tongue dancing with hers while their souls gave way to a thousand years of longing.

The closeness and the heat of their bodies was overwhelming. With the power of an earthquake, they cried out together. As his seed filled her, Malachi gathered Zilpah to him and held her close, breathing in that familiar and musky scent, knowing the aroma would forever have a different meaning. Suddenly reality came flooding back.

Malachi pulled away. He stood up, hands on his hips, scanning the room.

Zilpah gathered the bedclothes up around her.

"What is it?" she asked. "Why have you left me here? I thought things were going so well."

Malachi glared at her over his shoulder.

"Going well for who?" he barked. "For you?"

Zilpah smiled, her fangs gleaming in the candle light.

"Yes, for me." she said, licking her lips. "It is my triumph that you took me of your own free will."

"Oh, I see," Malachi began. "So, to the victor—"

"Go the spoils," Zilpah finished, shrugging her shoulders. "Of course."

Malachi walked to the small table and filled a chalice with the wine. Then holding it out, he smiled at Zilpah.

"Well then, you should drink to your vanquished enemy," Malachi said.

Zilpah shook her head playfully. "I have not had any drink but blood pass my lips since Ra changed me. And you are not my enemy, Malachi. You are my lover and my conquest."

Malachi pursed his lips and nodded.

"Alright, a compromise then."

"What did you have in mind?" she asked, eyebrows raised.

"A history lesson," he replied.

Malachi reached into his discarded clothes and pulled out a dagger. He made a small cut in the palm of his hand, then squeezed, allowing a stream of blood flow into the cup.

"An ancient nomadic tribe known as Scythians, took the 'spoils of war' most serious," he began. "A warrior was given the privilege of drinking the blood of his or her first 'conquest'."

While the wound on his hand healed itself, Malachi stirred his essence into the wine with his finger. Then he walked over to the bed and held out the chalice to Zilpah.

"You used the word, not me," he said handing her the cup. "So, drink. Take your place among the ancient warriors of Siberia."

Taking the cup, Zilpah eyed him with curiosity. That impish gleam that tugged at his nerves lit up her face. Zilpah raised the chalice to her nose, taking in the scent of Malachi's blood. Then holding the cup with both hands, she tilted it against her lips and swallowed down the whole thing. She let out a satisfied sigh as she tossed the empty vessel back to Malachi.

"Do you feel like a warrior?" he asked with a wink.

"I feel like I have conquered the highest mountain!" Zilpah shouted, throwing her arms in the air and flopping back into the bed pillows. "Or made love to a god."

Malachi chuckled as he sat the chalice back on the table. Then he walked back to the bed and climbed in beside her.

Zilpah leaned in to kiss his lips. As he turned away, she reared back.

"Why do you turn away from me?"

"I am no god," he replied with a smirk.

She leaned in and kissed his cheek, then moved down to the crook of his neck. For a moment, her tongue lingered there, while Zilpah contemplated plunging those perfect fangs into his vein.

"No," he whispered, taking her face in his hands. "I may be your conquest in bed, but I will not be food."

"You will never be just another meal to me, Malachi," Zilpah confessed, "or a conquest."

Her declaration inflamed his desire once more. Malachi pulled Zilpah close, wrapping his arms around her, possessing her with every fiber of his senses. He made love to her deep in to the night. Long after the candles had melted away.

Chapter Twenty-One

The Atlantic Ocean, The last week of September, 1592

Atargatis and Akhila breached in unison, their scales glimmering in the sun like prisms. The last three weeks had been some of the best of Akhila's life. Atargatis had proven herself to be a most trusted friend and a wise teacher.

Akhila flung her long hair back, sending a winged spray of sea water into the sky. She sighed heavily, drinking in the scent of the air, which had noticeably changed since approaching the Strait of Gibraltar. Her nostrils and her lungs filled with the heady aroma of foreign spices and the pollen of countless unknown flowers that drifted on the winds of the Mediterranean.

Being surrounded by newness, Akhila could feel the twinges of nervousness surfacing in her stomach. All of Atargatis's teachings would soon be put to the test.

"There," Atargatis called out, pointing ahead," The Straight. It is the only entrance to the great Mediterranean Sea."

Akhila swam up behind her teacher and lovingly wrapped her arms around Atargatis, locking her embrace across the sea goddess's upper chest. She peered around her teacher, and gazed upon the mouth of the straight.

"It is beautiful," Akhila sighed.

Atargatis returned the sentiment, reaching a webbed hand up out of the water and gently squeezed one of Akhila's wrists. Her heart softened a moment with the anticipation of seeing her sisters again. It had been far too long since Atargatis had visited with the sirens of the Leukai islands. She hoped they would feel the same.

"Is it much further to the islands?"

Atargatis's senses returned. Shrugging off Akhila's embrace, she turned and faced her with an ominous expression.

"When we enter the straight, you must follow me close," she warned. "Do not stray from my path. The waters of the straight are unique here. A mermaid can easily be pushed back out in to the open ocean for disrespecting the currents of the Mediterranean."

Akhila's smile faded as she gave Atargatis a single, solemn nod.

The two pushed against the water with their powerful tails and dove into the upper ocean current. Immediately the lighter, Atlantic flow carried them, and within moments, the Syrian goddess and the Mermaid of the Flint Place had traveled half the length of the strait of Gibraltar.

Akhila watched intently, mimicking every tail swoosh of Atargatis, careful not to stray from the path being mapped out before her. It had been one of Atargatis's first lessons. Know intimately every ebb and flow of the ocean. Her mermaid mind was quick to memorize the location of every current, their speeds, their shifts, even the minor temperature changes. Atargatis had stressed their importance. Every change mattered.

Like swords, the two pressed on, cutting through the water seamlessly. Then Atargatis dove deep, punching through the bottom of the Atlantic current, only to be scooped up by a heavier, opposing flow of water. Akhila followed suit, and soon the two were funneled through the back half of the straight and placed into the warm and salty arms of the Mediterranean Sea.

As the straight opened up into the sea, the currents slowed, dispersing their energies towards the endless shores that surrounded them. Once again the two mermaids broke the surface. As the warm Greek sun beamed down on Akhila's face, she suddenly felt a sense of home. A warmth ran through her, heating up her veins all the way down to the tips of her tail. The urge to be playful overtook her, and soon Akhila was diving and splashing like a child.

"Akhila, stop!" Atargatis shouted, chasing after her.

Seconds later, she was on top of the young mermaid, pushing her down under the water. When they were both submerged, Atargatis took a swipe at Akhila, slapping her square in the cheek.

"Foolish sprite!" she snarled. "Do you have any idea what would have happened if any humans had seen you?"

Akhila's lip pooched out as she rubbed her throbbing cheek.

"I was overcome," she replied. "It is so beautiful here."

Atargatis sighed. "Yes, my child, it is beautiful, but we must be on guard here. Fishermen would gladly skewer you on a harpoon and sell your carcass for an ounce of silver. Never trust the humans. We may be more powerful than they, but the souls of men are capable of unspeakable horror."

The young mermaid's face fell into a somber pout.

"Forgive me," Akhila whispered. "I still have much to learn."

"All is forgiven, Akhila of the Flint Place," Atargatis replied. "Come, let us continue. We shall stay under water til we reach The Pillar of Heracles."

The rest of the journey into the Mediterranean was silent and uneventful. Akhila drank in all she could of the ocean life that came and went from the mouth of the sea. As dusk began to pepper the sky with darkness, the two finally reached their destination. Atargatis motioned for Akhila to follow her up to the surface.

"Here we are," she decreed, bursting through the surface of the water. "When I was young, it was called 'The Pillar of Heracles.' But these more modern humans call it, the Rock of Gibraltar."

Akhila gazed up at the monstrous piece of limestone. At first, she marveled at its size and lovely shape. But it was the strange inhabitants she couldn't take her eyes off.

"Atargatis!" she cried. "What are those creatures, there on the cliffs?"

The sea goddess smiled. "The humans call them Barbary Apes. A tail-less type of animal, similar to men, found only on the pillar. They are the only beasts of its type found in this part of the world."

As the mermaids inched closer, many of the apes began to shift on the rock, pacing and staring out at them with interest. Then twelve stood up on their hind legs and dove into the sea, sinking to the now darkened depths and disappearing.

A squeal escaped Akhila's lips as she lunged forward.

"Why did they do that?" she asked. "Will they not be drowned?"

Bubbles began rising to the surface of the sea, a few at first, then thousands came rumbling out of the water, as if the Mediterranean itself were boiling. Then suddenly, twelve mermaids, donned with porcelain scales and creamy skin burst through the surf, surrounding Akhila and Atargatis like a wall of marble statues. A green-eyed siren glided up to Akhila, leaned in and sniffed her hair. As she pressed her nose into Akhila's locks, the siren murmured into her hear.

"We do not drown."

CHAPTER TWENTY-TWO

"Was your journey a safe one?" The Siren asked.

Akhila nodded slowly. "Y-yes it was."

"The waves were calm and smooth for travel?"

"Yes," Akhila answered again, her gaze falling warily on Atargatis, "we did not see a single storm."

The Siren smiled. Her teeth gleamed in the ever-brightening moonlight reflecting off the water. Slowly, she glided around and positioned herself behind Akhila. Then she leaned in once more, pressing her nose against the young mermaid's wet hair. The Siren inhaled another deep breath, drinking in Akhila's scent.

"You have not been at sea very long," the Siren hissed. "Your essence still stinks of dry land."

Akhila blushed and pulled away.

The other eleven began to chuckle under their breath as Akhila took shelter behind Atargatis.

"Thelxiepeia," Atargatis began.

"I have not heard that name in a long time," the Siren said. "Her highness has a good memory."

Atargatis smirked as she sized up the other eleven porcelain faces.

"Are your sisters all here with you?" she asked, "or did you finally make good on your threats and take your place as Melpomene's only daughter?"

Two Sirens hissed through the twilight.

"Ah, Peisinoe, Aglaope, there you are," Atargatis said, eying Thelxiepeia, "still with the living I see."

"Why have you come, goddess?" Thelxiepeia sighed. "Surely not to cause riffs in my family."

Atargatis scoffed. "Oh no, dear, you are more than capable of doing that yourself. No, no, we have come to witness the Turning of the Tide. You see, my young protege has yet to experience the ceremony."

"Well, you are fortunate to have come when you did," Thelxiepeia said with a nod. "We begin the ceremony when the last of the sun's rays have vanished from the sky."

Thelxiepeia turned and dove into water. The other eleven followed one at a time, their scales blending seamlessly with the moonlight. The Siren surfaced a few hundred yards away. Her mouth moved as if to speak.

"Follow me."

The words were no louder than a whisper, but were cradled in the wind, protected until they reached their destination.

Akhila glanced over at Atargatis.

"Should we follow her?" she asked.

"Oh yes, my dear," Atargatis replied. "If you do not, you will not learn all that the Sirens have to teach you."

The goddess and Akhila dove down into the water and began to follow the Sirens deep into the Strait of Gibraltar. Occasional fishing boats passed over head, casting shadows like wooden behemoths, while the lights from their lanterns illuminated even the tiniest creature living in the crystal-clear waters.

"You never told me," Akhila said, "who are the Sirens?"

"It is a tragic tale, Akhila," Atargatis replied.

"Please tell me?" the young mermaid pressed.

Atargatis nodded. "Very well. The three sisters were not always creatures of the sea. They donned lovely white wings. At the request of Hera, a goddess that lives on Mt. Olympus, Thelxiepeia and her sisters entered into a singing competition with the Muses—"

"Who are they?" Akhila interrupted.

"Theirs is the gift of artistic inspiration in men." Atargatis responded. "Do not interrupt me."

"Yes, ma'am," Akhila muttered.

"Anyway, The Sirens were no match for the Muses of Olympus. Their voices could not compete. Afterward the Muses plucked out their lovely white feathers and made crowns of them. Trophies. The Sirens, humiliated by the loss, turned pale with grief and fell into the sea, creating the Islands of Leukai... the White Ones."

Akhila shook her head.

"That is terrible."

"Do not waste your pity on those scornful vixens," Atargatis said. "They got exactly what they deserved. We all do in the end. Ah, look Akhila, the Islands of Leukai."

Akhila looked ahead and saw great piles of rock stacked into what appeared to be an altar. Dotted with corals and swirling with schools of fish, the altar at Leukai reminded Akhila of the palace of Poseidon. In the center stood a long, upright boulder, fitted with frayed ropes that swayed lazily in the current that shimmered in the lights coming off of the stars in the night sky. Akhila stopped and stared, her eyes wide, drinking in the natural beauty beneath the islands.

"It is even more lovely than I imagined," she whispered.

Thelxiepeia joined her.

"Yes it is," she said. "A labor of love. We come here every year and give offerings of peace to the tides."

Akhila smiled. "That is a beautiful sentiment. What do you offer?"

As the last word passed her lips, Akhila felt a sharp pain in the back of her head, then all was black.

Thelxiepeia reached out and grabbed a hold of Akhila's limp body with her free hand.

"You shall soon see," she replied dropping the rock clutched in her other fist.

CHAPTER TWENTY-THREE

The waters of the Mediterranean began to churn and swirl. Currents seemed to come alive, as if haunted by the power of the Siren's song. A curtain of bubbles rose from the blackened depths, carrying with them millions of silent, single-celled witnesses, there to oversee the Turning of the Tide.

Peisinoe, Aglaope and Thelxiepeia swayed in the fast-moving water, their voices in perfect harmony. On the sidelines, suspended in the water were the other nine Sirens and Atargatis, their voices not needed to appease the spirit of the ocean.

And there, tethered to the massive rock at the center of the altar, was Akhila. Her lifeless body bobbed like a buoy, straying from the altar only as far as the brittle ropes would allow.

While her sisters continued their song, Thelxiepeia broke away and swam to the center of the altar. She raised her hands towards the surface.

"Great spirit of the Tides," she called out, "We Sirens once again come to offer tribute to you. Through the offering of this lesser creature, permit us to live in harmony with you for another year."

Her pleas rang out into the water like a church bell. A thunderous roar responded from the blackness, sending vibrations through the water. The nine silent Sirens eyed each other with nervous glances. Then a black mass, whipping like a snake in the water, came rushing through the altar, pausing a moment in the center, then continuing to travel in and out in a continuous loop.

Atargatis swam to Thelxiepeia and grabbed her arm.

"Something is not right!" she growled. "The black current has never come before. What have you done?"

"This is not my doing." Thelxiepeia jerked away. "It is your presence here, goddess! Or maybe you brought us an offering that displeases the Spirit of the Tides. Where did this mermaid come from?"

Atargatis shrugged her shoulders. "She is no one of importance. Just some girl Poseidon spliced with a fish—"

"Poseidon?" Thelxiepeia screamed. "This girl is protected by Poseidon, and you brought her here to be *sacrificed?* Demon bitch, you have doomed us all!"

The Siren shoved Atargatis aside and rejoined her sisters in singing.

As the black mass swept past the center stone, it brushed Akhila's cheek. Akhila opened her eyes slowly, to the pandemonium that surrounded her. Fear rose in her throat as the dark current made another frantic pass. She looked on at the desperate Sirens, their eyes pinched shut while the song frantically continued to flowed from their lips.

"It is not enough," she said, "Their song is not enough."

Akhila took a deep breath.

"Please spirit," she whispered. "Do not be angry, let *me* sing you a song!"

The young mermaid closed her eyes and thought back to when she was a child. Her mother's voice rang in her ears, a beautiful voice offering love and reverence to the life giver- water. Akhila closed her eyes and let her mind wander, searching her memories for the words Bonsari used to sing.

"Ionkwanoronhkwa Ohneka
Ionkwanoronkhkwa Ohneka
Kahnekaronnion mmmm
Kahnekaronnion mmmm
Kainawiia Heiah
Yoon gwa no loon gwa
Oh ne gaw
Yoon gwa no loon gwa
Oh ne gaw
Gah ne gaw loonyoon mmmm
Gah ne gaw loonyoon mmmm
Guy naw wee yaw heh yaw..."

Like a charmed snake, the black current instantly slowed, then stopped moving. For several minutes it hung in the water, hypnotized by Akhila's voice. Then slowly, it weaved its way to her. With a feather-like touch, it flicked the end of its fleshless body, breaking the frayed cords that held Akhila's wrists.

While she continued to sing, the black current pitched and swayed in the water, occasionally spiraling around in a corkscrew, as if it were dancing on solid ground. Soon the Mermaid of the Flint Place joined in, singing and dancing a water waltz with the most powerful ocean current on earth.

Thelxiepeia opened her eyes. Her heart hardened as she watched Akhila and the ocean spirit. She took hold of each sister by the hand.

"After all these centuries," she snarled, her eyes still fixed on Akhila, "I will not allow some new fish to steal away the heart of the ocean spirit."

She let go of Peisinoe and Aglaope then started towards Akhila.

"Come," she called out," let us show her what a Siren's song can really do."

The three Sirens shot through the water like spears. Within seconds, Thelxiepeia and her sisters surrounded Akhila and began to sing. The ancient words pounded in Akhila's ears. The pain gripped at her mind, bringing forth every bad memory, every nightmare, every heartache. Akhila pressed her hands against the sides of her head, trying to keep out the lyrics.

"You think you can come here and woo the great ocean spirit with a song that like you, stinks of dry land?" Thelxiepeia spat. "You were brought here as a *sacrifice*, not as a bride!"

"P-please," Akhila whimpered, her consciousness fading, "stop, I beg you..."

Thelxiepeia glanced over her shoulder at Atargatis and the silent Siren. She smiled in triumph.

"Where is Poseidon?" she called out. "Where is the patron of this new fish?"

"I am here," a voice thundered from the current.

Thelxiepeia spun around. The ocean spirit had stopped its dancing and while the Siren was gloating, had positioned itself between her and Akhila. Its endless snake-like body began to swell, enclosing the new three sisters in coils of a black watery void.

"You are not Poseidon," the Siren hissed.

"I never said I was," the current boomed. "It matters not, your insolence will not be tolerated,"

A whip of black water shot out from the current, slashing at the silent sirens. A burst of light exploded from each of them, as one by one the magic that encapsulated them popped like balloons. When the whip retracted, all that was left were nine drowned monkeys from the Pillar of Heracles.

"NO!" Thelxiepeia cried. "My lovelies, they were innocents! Why not take the girl we offered you?"

"Yes," the current rumbled. "I will."

Another extension of blackened water reached out, this time forming a hollow vortex, swirling and channeling like the funnel of a tornado. Slowly it stretched out to the altar where Akhila was floating. The funnel's suction latched on, pulling her towards the opening. As her body inched closer to the opening, it picked up speed. Then in one final gulp, Akhila of the Flint Place disappeared into the darkness of the slipstream.

CHAPTER TWENTY-FOUR

The Underworld, June, 1593

"Your servant confessed to it, Hades!" Malachi bellowed, slamming his fist on the dining table. "It has been nearly nine months to the day."

"I know," Hades replied. "Soon Malachi, soon. The Fates will let us know when the child is to arrive."

"Damn the Fates!" Malachi fired back. "In life Balthazar took his marching orders from Yahweh. He would want me to act, now. Not sit around here waiting on the whims of pagan witches."

Hades's jaw tightened at the mention of the Most High's name. He turned away, squeezing his eyes shut.

Malachi leaned in. "What? Does His name pain you? Can you not stand to be in the presence of His name passing through my lips?"

Hades turned back and faced Malachi, a snarl curling his lip.

"No!" he fired back. "I cannot. Are you satisfied?"

Malachi's face softened. He leaned back in his chair once more.

"Forgive me," he mumbled. "That was cruel. I am no more in His Good Graces than you."

Hades nodded. "All is forgiven. You are traveling in

circles that are very different from mine. I forgot to respect that. If you feel it is time, then go. If the child has been born, retrieve him and bring him back here. The Fates will be arriving soon. Then we can right this wrong."

Malachi slid his chair back and rose from the table.

"I will take Ruki with me and leave within the hour."

"Take care young Sand Dweller," Hades replied. "Within the walls of Hell you will not find passive servants or friendly faces. The inhabitants of Perdition cannot be trusted like they can here."

Malachi snorted and rolled his eyes.

"The underworld is solely inhabited by men who have nothing left to lose," Malachi replied. "None of them can be trusted, not really."

He turned on his heel and walked out of the banquet hall. As he passed the threshold, Malachi looked to his right and found Ruki sitting on the floor, resting his arms across his knees.

"He does not want you to go," Ruki said.

"No," Malachi replied. "But he will not stop me."

"He will try," Ruki whispered, rising to his feet.

"Yes," Malachi said, "But that is all he will do."

CHAPTER TWENTY-FIVE

Hell

Uphir's arm swung wide, the back of his hand striking Zilpah in the cheek.

"Push the little bastard out, stupid woman!" he bellowed, slapping her again.

"Will you stop!" Zilpah fired back, clutching her red face. "I am doing the best I can."

Hell's physician turned his back to her. With his clawed hands clasped behind his back, Uphir paced around the bed, grumbling under his breath.

"This would not be a problem for a *real* demon," he sneered. "Of all the creatures under earth, he had to lay with you—"

Uphir paused and glared at Zilpah.

"—an abomination of our kind."

Zilpah lurched forward as the contraction ripped through her lower back.

"Arrrrgggg........," she cried out. "I am not an abomination!"

Uphir chuckled.

"Tell me whore, what did you have to do to get Azazael's son to willingly leave his seed in your rotten womb?"

As the pains subsided, Zilpah's cheeks ballooned. She

let out a breath, then absently, drug the back of her arm across her forehead, clearing away the numerous beads of sweat that had accumulated there. Then she leaned back against a mountain of pillows stacked up behind her.

"You are just jealous," she spat. "I will forever be affiliated with one of the most powerful demons in Hell, and you will remain just as you are. A nursemaid. Lucifer's bitch!"

With a roar, Uphir stormed back around the bed. He grabbed Zilpah's throat and began to squeeze. As her air supply diminished, Zilpah's face turned purple and bloated.

"I am he who touched your mother in the night, striking her down with leprosy," he growled. "The whisper of fire in Nero's ear. I can fill Charon's ferry with souls by just thinking it!"

The physician released his grip on Zilpah's neck. As she coughed and gasped for air, Uphir continued.

"I am not just a doctor," he said, "what I do shakes the very foundations of the earth. I forge man's history with death and disease, I can fill his lungs with poison just as easily as air. I am no warrior, it is true. I do not run in to battle shaking my fists and waving around swords. But when I strike to kill, it is not one at a time. I murder legions."

Another contraction began to well up inside. Zilpah grabbed a hold of the sides of the bed and braced herself. The pain exploded in her back, tying her muscles in knots with every cramp.

"Enough talk!" Uphir yelled in her face. "Push that brat out of your overused twat before I rip him out!"

Leaning forward once more, Zilpah strained with all her strength. Her opening stretched and tore, shooting a stabbing pain up into her stomach. She pinched her eyes shut and strained even more.

"Yes!" Uphir yelled. "Push harder, you whore! Here he comes."

With the last of her strength, Zilpah gave one final push. It was enough. The newborn's head broke free of his mother, followed by the rest of his body. Zilpah looked down between her legs. There in the bloody bedclothes, lay a child. Hers and Malachi's child. The boy squirmed and twisted, his hands pawing at the air. A smile raised one side of her mouth.

"Now we will always be connected," she whispered, caressing the boy's fuzzy head. "My conquest, my lover..."

"That is quite enough," Uphir said. "I suggest you not get too attached to that boy."

Zilpah looked up, her eyes piercing Hell's physician.

"What is that supposed to mean?"

"You do not actually believe that the general will allow you to raise his grandson, do you?" Uphir cracked.

"He will not take my son!" Zilpah fired back. "He would not dare!"

Uphir leaned down and picked up the child by an ankle. He held the dangling newborn at eye level, gave the child one quick swat on the backside and then began inspecting him. Casually, he took hold of the umbilical cord, then with one bite, chewed through it, severing the baby from his mother. Then turning the child around, Uphir's eyes fell on a tiny pair of featherless wings protruding from the child's back.

"Oh my word," he muttered. "What do we have here?"

Zilpah tilted her head to one side. "What are you looking at? What is wrong with him?"

The physician calmly walked to the door and stuck his head out.

"Come in here,"

A small soul hesitantly stepped in. "Yes, Doctor?"

Uphir handed the child off to the soul, then wiped his hands on the folds of his cloak.

"There is a cage with fresh skins prepared in my chambers," Uphir said. "Take the child there."

"No!" Zilpah cried, lunging forward.

"Silence, whore!" he growled.

The soul cradled the child against its chest, bowed to the demon then exited the room.

"I shall be going to the surface for a few days," Uphir said, "on business. Use the time to get yourself cleaned up and healed up. Azazael will want to see you and the child when I get back."

Uphir turned and opened the chamber door.

"If you try to take the child, the general will hunt you like a beast. He is the Watcher of War. There is no place in Hell or on earth you could possibly hide. Heed my warning."

As Hell's Physician stepped into the corridor, Zilpah's screams followed him out like a mist. He breathed them in like a sweet perfume, then marched off into the darkness.

CHAPTER TWENTY-SIX

The Gates of Hell

The Samurai and the Sand Dweller maneuvered the darkened tunnels that connected the various realms of the underworld in silence. Occasionally a random gate or doorway would appear, sparking a brief commentary by Ruki. Malachi listened with interest, absorbing the information as though he were a sightseer on some macabre tour.

As the pair rounded a sharp corner, the temperature shifted. Stiff, chilly gusts of wind whipped and festered, kicking up the dust under their feet and bending the fire in the wall sconces to their limits. There in a high vaulted clearing, stood a pair of iron gates. Beyond them, a winding frozen road burrowed into an expanse of a seemingly open sky, snow drifts and ridged mountains.

"Where does that road lead?" Malachi asked, pulling his cloak tighter.

"That road leads to Helheim," Ruki said, "the dead there are ruled by the goddess, Hel."

Malachi frowned. "Hel?"

"She is said to be the daughter of Loki, who is the son of Odin, who is the ruler of Asgard."

"Sounds complicated," Malachi said.

"It is," Ruki agreed. "Hel is a two-faced goddess, half

is youthful and eternally beautiful, while the other half is dead and decayed. It is believed that when a Norseman dies, Hel will judge him upon arrival. His paradise or his damnation begin immediately."

Malachi shivered. "She does not waste any time."

"Indeed she does not," Ruki said.

They resumed their silence and pushed on, leaving the blizzards of Helheim behind them. Malachi sighed heavily. The bitter winds of the Norse underworld reminded him of Zilpah. Like the snow and wind, she was cold and would sting with her cruelty. His thoughts went back to that night. The vacant dent she left in his bed was more frigid than anything the landscape of Helheim could muster.

"You are thinking about her,"

Malachi shrugged his shoulders.

"You are confused,"

Malachi shook his head. "No, I can see clearly."

"Why are we venturing into the blackest pit?" Ruki asked.

"To retrieve a soulless child." Malachi answered.

"Why?"

"So I can free Balthazar's soul from the defixio," Malachi said with a frown. "You know all of this already."

Ruki stopped and faced Malachi. He placed his hands on the Sand Dweller's shoulders then peered deep into his eyes.

"And why is that task necessary?" Ruki pressed.

Malachi glared back at Ruki. The samurai was right. He had allowed the soft curves and purring voice of Zilpah to cloud his mind. She had not used her magic on him that night, and yet he felt just as bewitched as he had in Scotland. He shook his head.

"I do not know how to feel," he said. "We have shared a bed. Why is it so hard to hate her now?"

"She is a beautiful creature," Ruki said. "The female of our species always has the upper hand. They do not need dark magic to direct a man's soul. You will have to work extra hard and never forget the reason you are here."

Malachi smiled and turned back to face Ruki. He reached up with his own hands and grabbed on to Ruki's shoulders.

"What would I do without you?"

Ruki smiled and gave Malachi a wink.

"Down here?" he said. "You would literally be lost without me. Come on now, our destination is just up around the next bend in the road."

The air around them began to change. Helheim's frozen winds had been replaced by the stench of sulfur and the hot breath of damnation. Malachi stripped off his heavy cloak and tossed it on the ground against the rocky wall.

"We are here," Ruki said, pointing at the gate. "The bottom rung of the underworld. Hell."

The hell hound that guarded the heavy iron gate paced and growled as the two drew closer. Several pairs of glowing red eyes appeared in the blackness that lay beyond the entrance, staring out with curiosity and fear. The beast took a defensive stance, blocking the rusted latch that prevented Hell's doomed inhabitants from escape.

Ruki instinctively drew his katana.

"No," Malachi said, raising a hand. "Let me,"

Malachi approached the hell hound. He stared into the creatures eyes a moment, searching. Deep inside his head, a memory began to stir, a memory that was not his own. As it festered, flashes of images began to assault his mind. Malachi saw himself ripping away the flesh of the hell hound, exposing the true beast within. His eyes began to glow, giving Malachi the demon sight.

"You are no hell hound," Malachi roared. "End this farce. Show your true self!"

The creature stood up on its hind legs and howled, sending an ear-piercing call deep into the underworld. Its front paws began to stretch and twist, shifting from canine, to semi-human. When its paws had become hands and feet, the hell hound began frantically ripping at its flesh, peeling off bloody strips of fur and skin. Within a few minutes, the beast's facade was gone, leaving behind a bloody, naked and furious demon.

"You sanctimonious bastard!" the demon cursed. "Do you have any idea how much it hurts to peel that skin off? I should cut your throat!"

Malachi shook his head. "But you will not. Let us pass."

The naked demon took a step towards Malachi.

"Why should I? I do not know you, you do not know me."

"You are Malik," Malachi sneered, his eyes blazing red. "To the Akkadians you were a prince, to the Arabs you are an angel king. But to Lucifer, you are just a lowly gatekeeper who hides behind the skin of a dog."

Malik's mouth dropped open.

"How do you know me?" he snarled. "Who are you?"

"I am Malachi Ben Sinai, son of Azazael. Now, let us pass!"

With the mention of the general's name, Malik's face fell in defeat. With his head hung, he walked to the gate and unhooked the latch. He gave the heavy gate a yank, its ancient hinges protesting with every step. When the gate was open, Malik peered into the blackness.

"Make way for the General's son!" he bellowed. "Let him pass."

Malik turned back and glared at Malachi.

"Enjoy your stay," he said with a smirk.

Malachi returned the glare then stepped across the threshold of Hell's gate. He glanced to either side of him and found nineteen armored guards standing at attention, all sporting a pair of red glowing eyes. Malachi looked back at Ruki and beckoned him.

"Come on, it is safe,"

As Ruki started towards the entrance, Malik leaned in close to his ear.

"Famous last words," he chuckled. "Getting in will prove much easier than getting back out."

CHAPTER TWENTY-SEVEN

"It is not often one finds a gatekeeper with so much charm," Ruki observed. "How did you know the hell hound was truly a demon? I have been a guide in Yomi for centuries and never knew that little secret."

Malachi shrugged his shoulders. "I cannot say for sure. Sometimes the curse of my father will surface. Most of the time it just robs me of my reason and makes me rage like an animal. This is the first time it has ever been helpful."

"Huh," Ruki sighed. "Perhaps it is your proximity to Hell. I imagine the power is stronger when you are close to the source. Speaking of which, do you suppose this curse will point the way to Zilpah and the child?"

Malachi searched his mind once more. The images were faint and muddied with a kind of black fog. He squeezed his eyes shut and concentrated. As his hands rose to his temples, massaging the now bulging veins in the side of his face, a voice, just as faint as the images came through.

"Here your path's must part," it whispered. *"But you will meet again. It is crucial that your hands alone deliver the child from Lucifer's claw. The samurai will be in no danger. "*

He stole a sideways glance at his new ally. So noble and devoted. Malachi knew the voice was right. As it had always done, the curse would take away another trusted companion. The weight of fate hung heavy in the pit of his stomach.

"There is nothing," Malachi lied. "But, I think we should split up. Whichever one of us finds the child will take him out of Hell and deliver him to Hades."

Ruki shook his head. "I am not sure that is wise—"

"Please!" Malachi shouted.

His outburst gave Ruki a start.

"What is it?" Ruki asked. "Why do you insist on dividing our resources?"

Malachi shook his head. "I cannot say for sure. Just please, we *must* split up. We will cover more ground this way."

"All right," Ruki conceded. "This is your mission. We will do it your way."

"Thank you," Malachi said. "You are a good friend."

The tunnel was long and black, save the occasional sconce filled with hell fire. Doors appeared at random, some made of wood, others of stone, while some openings in the tunnel walls had no door at all.

As they traveled deeper into Hell, a wide, circular clearing emerged, its walls smooth as blackened glass and adorned with mounted iron shackles. Several sets of the ferrule bracelets held unwilling souls. At the sight of Ruki and Malachi, the captive souls began wailing and begging to be released.

"Should we set them free?" Ruki asked.

Malachi shook his head. "No, it is too late for mercy. In life they all did something to deserve being sent here. They reached for death when they should have been reaching for God. Look at them. Even now that death has them in its grasp, they do not think to cry out to God, the only One who could possibly save them. That is why they will never leave here."

"Your God would come into the realm of Lucifer and save these souls?" Ruki asked.

"I do not know," Malachi admitted. "It would take the one thing that is missing in this place. Hope. I noticed it when we first crossed the threshold. You cannot feel the tug of hope."

"So, Virgil was right," Ruki muttered.

Malachi raised an eyebrow.

"Who is Virgil?"

"He is another who guides those who visit the underworld," Ruki replied with a chuckle. "He tells everyone he meets to abandon all hope. Now I know why."

Reginald and his nervousness about entering the Ogre in Bomarzo flooded into Malachi's thoughts. A brief pang of jealousy pressed on his stomach. Mortal men it would seem were much more in tune with the spiritual world than he realized.

A roar echoed into the clearing, followed by heavy, thundering footfalls. Something large and angry was coming from the left tunnel. As the growls and snarls grew louder, the damned chained to the wall began to frantically twist and tug at their shackles

"I think we need to hide," Malachi said, snapping to attention.

Quickly, the two ducked into the darkness of the right tunnel and waited. Seconds later, a massive Nephilim came lumbering into the clearing, its meaty neck turning its half-rotted head back and forth, while hollow eye sockets pretended to scan the space for food. The giant tilted its head back and sniffed the air, then let out another roar.

The shackled souls cowered in terror. In the tongues of their former lives, the captives begged for mercy while jerking at their restraints.

The sound of metal on stone was like a homing beacon. The Nephilim turned and faced the direction of the rattling chains. It reached out with bloody claws and ripped one of the souls off the wall. With a ravenous snarl, it bit a large chunk out of the soul's thigh and began chewing.

"Horrible," Ruki whispered. "I cannot bear to watch,"

"This is not the worst of it," Malachi replied.

Ruki's mouth hung open, "What could be worse than being eaten alive?"

"These souls are not being consumed," Malachi whispered back. "When my cousin in there has had its fill, the soul will remain."

"Cousin?" Ruki asked

Malachi nodded. "Those souls will be eaten alive every day. For all time. Their torment will never end."

He paused a moment, then pointed at the Nephilim. "Watch,"

The beast devoured the last chunks of the soul. Then it felt around on the floor, scraping up any pieces that may have escaped its lips. When nothing remained but pools of blood, bone and bits of gristle, the Nephilim belched and lumbered off into the blackness of the tunnel.

Ruki cautiously poked his head out into the clearing.

"What am I supposed to see?" he asked.

The bloody floor began to churn and bubble. Ruki let out a gasp as the left-over bits and pools of blood began to creep on their own towards the now empty shackles hanging on the wall. Forming a solid mass, the sticky substance crept up the wall, all the while stretching and expanding until at last the consumed soul was once again whole and hanging by its eternal restraints.

Ruki stepped back into the tunnel and leaned against wall, squeezing his eyes shut.

"What did I just witness?" he whispered. "It defies all reason... all sanity."

"I know," Malachi said. "The choices we make in life, will ring out like a gong in our afterlife. These unfortunates will never rest. That is why there is no point in trying to help them."

Ruki opened his eyes.

"Why did you call that creature your cousin?"

"Because it is," Malachi said with a shrug. "They are called Nephilim. Children born of human mothers and—"

"Demon fathers?" Ruki asked.

Malachi nodded. "At the time of their birth, their fathers were angels, but yes."

"Why then, do you not look like these 'Nephilim'?"

"Because they embraced the darkness of the world," Malachi answered. "They chose hate and wrath to be their guides. It is the reason they are here. When they were living beings, they allowed their hate to fester until they had murdered each other. I do not and will not allow the curse of my birth to rule me."

Ruki grasped Malachi by the shoulder and gave it a squeeze.

"I hope you succeed," he said.

"First things first," Malachi said. "We must find the child. Take this tunnel. I shall take the tunnel the Nephilim came from."

"Is it safe?" Ruki asked.

"Of course," Malachi replied with a wink. "They will not harm me. I am family."

Ruki shook his head and smiled.

"At least you have a sense of humor about it."

"Do not wait for me," Malachi said. "If you find the child, take him to Hades."

"Consider it done," Ruki said.

Malachi stepped back into the clearing. Then he turned back to his friend once more.

"May the Lord Bless you, Ruki Nagamatsu," he called out.

"And you as well, Malachi Ben Sinai," Ruki replied from the darkness. "Koketsu ni irazunba koji wo ezu."

CHAPTER TWENTY-EIGHT

"**M**erciful Father, bless thy humble servant, a lowly and damned sinner. Look upon thy condemned follower with compassion, for thy servant was not wholly willing to rebel against thee. Thy humble servant comes to thee on bended knees, eternally penitent, and will faithfully wait upon thee for all time. Show thy servant the way to Salvation, place the feet of thy servant upon the road on which thou wishes thy servant to tread. The road to forgiveness. The road that leads thy servant back to the gates of Heaven. Forever will thy servant listen for thy voice, oh Lord. Amen."

Abbadona rose from a well-worn and deeply dented cushion that formed the base of the small alter in his quarters. He reached across the top of the alter to a large candle. The demon licked his forefinger and thumb, then before the fires of Hell could evaporate the wetness, Abbadona pinched the flaming wick, snuffing out its golden light. Then grabbing up a stack of tomes, the demon made his way across the chambers to a large stone desk. As he plopped down in the chair, a cautious knock vibrated from his chamber door.

"You may enter," Abbadona called out.

A soul nervously entered the chambers, its arms loaded with several scrolls.

"Ah!" Abbadona said, clasping his hands with joy. "They have arrived. Quickly, bring them here, bring them here!"

The soul scurried up to the desk and piled the scrolls up in front of the excited demon.

"Did you have any trouble getting them down here?" he asked, rifling through the pile.

"No my lord," the soul replied. "I used the spell you gave me. Malik did not smell them, just as you said."

Abbadona smile widened. "Good, that is very good,"

"But, my lord," the soul said, "I am afraid there is a small problem."

The demon looked up from the scroll he was unrolling. "A problem?"

"Y-yes, you see—"

Abbadona reached out and took the nervous soul by the hand.

"What was your name in life?" he asked.

"My people called me Gregor, my lord."

"Well, Gregor," the demon said, "you need not fear me as you fear the others. What ever the problem is, I am sure it is not as bad as you think."

Gregor let out a relieved sigh.

"You see my lord, the scribes would not let me have the originals."

Abbadona nodded once. "I see. Continue."

"So," Gregor said, "I was forced to make copies instead."

The demon finished unrolling the scroll in his hand and looked it over.

"So, you wrote these?" he asked.

"Yes my lord," Gregor replied. "The mystics insisted, sir. They did not believe I was a condemned soul from Hell. Also, they did not believe in you, sir."

Abbadona laughed and leaned back in his chair. A penitent demon. Who in their right mind would believe in such an absurd creature? He stood up and walked around to the front of the desk.

"Gregor, you have done extremely well," Abbadona said. "Your copies are perfectly transcribed. As far as I am concerned, they are just as good as originals. Thank you."

The soul let out another sigh of relief. It had been fifty years since Gregor had died. A penniless drunk, he had taken to the streets, using any means necessary to secure the coin needed to fill his belly with ale. In life, Gregor never much cared who he raped, beat or killed to get the money. All that mattered was that he get it. And when the drink he loved finally took the last breath from his lungs, Gregor discovered the terrible price he was to pay for all of the lives he stole. Gregor Daniel Jacobs woke up from death in Hell.

"Thank you my lord," Gregor said, a faint smile forming at the corners of his mouth. "You have no idea how much your kindness means to me. Will you be needing anything else from me, sir?"

Abbadona shook his head. "No no, I think that will be all, for now. Perhaps I will call upon you for another task soon."

Gregor's face fell. "As you wish, sir."

The disappointed soul turned and walked to the door. As he stepped out into the hallway, the usual sounds of pain and torment rang in his ears. Gregor took a deep breath. The weight of Hell's fury began to press down on his shoulders. He wondered as he shuffled down the corridor, what suffering would befall him next. The anxiety of being a servant soul was horrific. Each demon had a different appetite when it came to torture. Gregor shuttered as he thought of his next assignment.

A silhouette emerged from the darkness. Silent and quick, the figure closed the distance between them in moments. Gregor could see that it was a man adorned in armor. The light from a nearby sconce reflected the stranger's sword.

As stranger approached him, Gregor pressed his back to the wall and pinched his eyes shut. He had learned early on, that it was best to just submit to whatever whim was in the demon's blackened hearts.

He stood there for several minutes, waiting.

"Are you all right?"

Gregor cautiously opened one eye.

The stranger stood before him, a curious and worrisome look on his face.

"I said, are you all right?"

The soul opened his other eye and let his shoulders relax.

"Yes," he answered, "as well as can be expected, sir."

The stranger nodded. "Good. Tell me, do you know where I can find Zilpah's living quarters?"

Gregor sucked in a breath and shook his head.

"N-no," he stuttered. "But my master may be able to help you."

Gregor turned and walked back to Abbadona's door. He knocked twice and then waited for permission to enter.

The demon's voice beckoned him in.

"Why, Gregor," Abbadona said. "I am surprised to see you back so soon. What is it?"

"There is someone outside that needs to see you," Gregor said.

"Who is it?" Abbadona asked, rising from his desk.

"I do not know, my lord," Gregor replied. "He does not appear to be a resident of Hell."

CHAPTER TWENTY-NINE

The tell-tale crack of a bullwhip rang out from the blackness, followed by a faint whimper. The whip struck again and again, while the woman's voice grew more gravely and dry, begging for mercy between lashes. Then there was laughter, followed by more whipping. Slowly, the begging became moaning, then the moaning turned into cries of ecstasy. But, then the abuse came full circle, and soon the mysterious woman was wailing in agony once more.

Malachi winced as the screams of the woman pierced his eardrums like hot irons. When the lashing stopped, he froze mid-stride, listening. The cries had stopped. Up ahead, a glowing red beam of light flooded out from an open door. The Sand Dweller inched his way along the wall, his eyes focused on the light.

Random clacking of metal on metal echoed out from the open door. One particular voice from inside the chamber was guttural and savage.

"Clamp her down,"

"Yes, my lord,"

"Now flip her,"

"Yes, my lord,"

"Good, now, put it in her mouth,"

"Yes, my lord,"

As Malachi approached the entrance, a new series of

whip cracks echoed out into the corridor. He took a deep breath and peered into the doorway. There, two souls hung in the center of the room, one from her ankles and one from his wrists. The demon in charge had chained them together, their faces pressed into one another's genitals. As the two condemned swung back and forth, the demon flogged them, leaving it to chance on whom the lashes would land.

While the demon's back was too the door, Malachi walked past, stopping a moment to glance in. His eyes met the worn and defeated face of a servant soul, who stood silently by awaiting commands from his taskmaster. As their gazes locked, Malachi could physically feel the hopelessness and misery radiating out of the poor unfortunate. It burrowed deep into his brain and for just a moment, Malachi could see all the wrong this former man had done. Every rotten sin that tainted every thought, word and deed that had come from him while he had been living. The weight of this soul's sins were too much. Malachi quickly looked away and moved on.

The corridor grew silent, as torture rooms were slowly replaced by living quarters. Most of the doors were shut and marked with the occupant's sigil. Malachi recognized most of the symbols from hours of pouring over scrolls and ancient tomes with Balthazar. He smiled to himself as he pulled Balthazar's journal from his pocket. Half way through, he found the sigil he needed. A four-legged insect-like figure, its back legs reminiscent of iron crosses, while the front feet were cast as simple circles.

"Ba'al," Malachi whispered, closing the journal.

"Not that one," a voice called out.

Malachi spun around and came face to face with the servant soul from the torture room. The servant's eyes darted up and down the corridor, his nervous hands wringing and tugging on his ragged tunic.

"Ba'al does not have the child, my lord," the servant whispered.

Then he reached out and took the journal from Malachi's hand. He flipped through a few pages, then smiled.

"This one, my lord," the servant said, handing back the open journal. "You need to go and see the doctor."

Malachi glanced down at the page and quickly memorized the sigil. Then he closed the journal and stuffed it back into his pocket. When he looked back up, the servant was gone.

He broke into a jog, quickly scanning door after door. Then just before he reached a bend in the corridor, he found it. Malachi stood before the splintered wooden entrance, staring down the branded symbol that adorned the chamber door of Uphir. He reached out and yanked on the iron ring, releasing the latch on the other side. The wooden door swung in easily and silently, revealing the dwelling place of Hell's Physician.

Malachi stepped across the threshold, his eyes darting around the room. There in a far corner, tucked in amongst stacks of books and piles of bone was a small cage. As he inched closer, Malachi could see the bottom of the cage was lined with layers of animal skins and laying right on top, was the child. The boy, only hours old, lay stoic, as if lost in deep thought.

He reached down and carefully picked up the boy,

along with a rabbit skin. Then he swaddled up the newborn, tucked him and the skin up under his tunic and ran back out into the corridor.

CHAPTER THIRTY

"This is highly unusual," Abbadona said, motioning to a chair. "Most people are trying to get out of Hell, not break in."

Ruki sat down.

"Yes, I imagine my being here would seem strange. But, I have been sent here on a mission from Hades. I am sure you can appreciate the importance of that."

Abbadona leaned forward and rested his forearms on the desk.

"Really?" he asked. "And how is the eldest child of the all powerful Chronos?"

Ruki smiled. "He is well. My companion and I are here to retrieve the newborn child of Zilpah—"

"Your companion?" Abbadona said, gazing wide eyed at the door. "There is another here with you?"

"Yes," the samurai answered, "Malachi, a half demon from the surface."

Abbadona lurched forward in his chair.

"Are you here with General Azazael's son? Where is he?"

"We parted ways at the clearing near the gate," Ruki replied. "Malachi felt we could cover more ground if we searched on our own. Please, can you tell me where I can find Zilpah's child?"

"Ah yes, the infant born with no soul," Abbadona

sighed. "He was birthed earlier today. The servant souls and lower demons can speak of nothing else. It seems one of ours has become a grandfather."

Abbadona frowned, losing himself in thought, then chuckled to himself.

"What is it?" Ruki asked.

"Oh, it is just fascinating to me, that even on the road to Perdition, a newborn babe can still inspire and excite."

Abbadona stood up and paced the room, his clawed hands clasped behind his back. He muttered under his breath as he stopped and gazed out the window, a window that looked down on the east end of the great wall that surrounded Lucifer's palace.

"What did you say?" Ruki said, joining him at the window. "I did not catch that."

"Mother and child would be in the west wing," Abbadona said. "No doubt delivered by Uphir. Azazael's son could be in danger if he is discovered there alone. He has many enemies in Hell."

Ruki pulled the hood of his cloak back over his head and started for the door.

"I know pairing back up was not a part of Malachi's plan, but I must go to him,"

"Yes," Abbadona said, "Should he come across Zilpah's patron,"

Ruki nodded and jerked open the door.

"Thank you,"

"You are welcome, Samurai," Abbadona said. "I will be praying for your safety."

CHAPTER THIRTY-ONE

The shore of the River Styx

Charon docked his boat at the end of the ancient pier and waited. He glanced up at the perpetual night above him, scanning for streaks of light. On the surface, humans marveled at the beauty and mystery of falling stars. But on the river banks of the underworld, those streaks in the sky were no celestial bodies. Instead, they represented the souls of condemned men, falling from grace. Cast down, these eternally lost sheep would wander the border between the living and the dead. Wander until they came to the river.

The ancient boat creaked and moaned in protest. Ripples formed on the normally still surface of the river, gently lapping against the wood. The ferryman leaned over the side, then cast his gaze out towards the shore. There, washed up on the blackened silt lay an unconscious mermaid. Her long silver tail, still partially in the river, swayed back and forth, sending out a steady stream of pulses on the water.

Charon pulled his long oar out of the river. He flipped it paddle side up, allowing the water run down the length of the shaft. As the paddle dried, it began to bend and warp, forming the head of a scythe. Armed and curious, the ferryman stepped out of the boat onto the rickety pier, then made his way to shore.

When he reached the mermaid, she was still out cold, though her tail continued to sway in the water, as if it were trying to pull the rest of her back into the drink. Charon watched for a moment, then gently pressed the end of his scythe into the mermaid's ribs and gave her a jab.

"You," Charon called out, "rise from your slumber and state your business on my river."

The mermaid slowly opened her eyes and looked up. The sight of Charon, a living skeleton, shrouded in long gray rags and wielding a blackened scythe gripped her. She quickly rolled over onto her back and began to scoot backwards.

"Are you Onyare?" her voice quivered. "Have you come to kill me?"

Charon snickered behind his tatters and sat the end of the scythe on the ground like a walking staff.

"No, fish girl," he replied, holding out his hand, "I am not."

The mermaid's shoulders lowered slightly, the tension easing in her muscles.

"Then, who are you?" she asked. "And what is this place?"

"I am Charon, the Ferryman. I ferry souls who have left their bodies across the river to the land of the dead. There, they are led by guides to their final resting place."

Charon turned and pointed to the distant shore on the other side of the river.

"There, you see," he said, "That is the entrance to the underworld."

The mermaid pulled herself all the way up onto the

dry shore, her muscular tail immediately splitting into a pair of long, bronze legs. A faint smile lifted the corners of her mouth. Akhila was getting better at controlling the change. She stood up and faced the ferryman with pride and bravery glinting in her eyes.

"I am Akhila, Mermaid of the Flint Place," she declared. "There was some trouble... the ocean spirit rescued me from the Sirens,"

"Really?" Charon started, "Do tell,"

Akhila nodded. "Well, I was in some kind of magic sleep. It took me deep into its current. When I awoke, I was here."

Charon nodded, the brittle vertebrate in his neck creaking like an old hinge.

"I wonder why Poseidon deposited you here," he said.

"Oh no!" Akhila said, "I have met the great god of the sea, this was something different,"

Again, the ferryman let loose with a snicker.

"My child, Poseidon can take many forms. He must have a special interest in you."

"He bonded me with the river father," Akhila replied. "This is why I now dwell in the sea."

"Well," Charon said, "that makes him your patron. He must have a reason for bringing you here. Perhaps he is sending you on an errand to the land of the dead. If you have payment, I can take you across."

Akhila shook her head.

"If that is true, why would he not tell me what he wants me to do here?"

Charon turned and glided back down the pier.

"That is not known to me, Akhila and frankly, I do not

care. The gods are strange creatures. Make your decision, I shall be waiting in the boat."

He stepped back onto the ferry. Then twirling the scythe like a staff, Charon plunged the bladed end into the river. Reunited with the waters of the Styx, the head of the scythe shifted back into the paddle end of an oar.

Akhila stood on the pier, her eyes darting back and forth between the ferryman and the shore of the underworld that awaited her across the river. She thought back to the dreams she had, the fire, the roar of thunder. Akhila knew deep down within herself that this was where she was supposed to be. It wasn't Poseidon or an ocean spirit that had brought her to the very doorstep of the dead. It was fate.

"Are you coming?" Charon called out from the boat.

"Yes," she answered, walking to the end of the pier. "But I am afraid I do not have anything to pay you."

"That strand of beads," Charon called out, pointing his bony finger at her mother's necklace. "Is it valuable to you?"

Akhila reached up and grasped the necklace. Her heart sank. The necklace was the only part of her human life she could take with her. With shaky fingers, she untied the sinew cord and dropped the strand into Charon's outstretched hand.

"I accept your payment," he said, "you have my permission to board my ferry."

Akhila stepped onto the boat, her bare feet padding across the weathered deck, carrying her to the bow. There she stood, silent, her hands gripping the splintered railing and staring at the shore across the river. The pangs of fear began to well within her.

The ferryman took his place at the stern. With his bony fingers wrapped around the oar, Charon began to paddle, using long strokes. Akhila's beaded necklace clinked and jingled, broke the silence with its pinging against the oar with every stroke.

Glancing over her shoulder, Akhila stole a glimpse of the ferryman. Her eyes panned down to the dangling string of beads in his hand and could feel herself growing angry. The salmon began to stir inside her, firing off pulses in the nerves running up and down her legs. Absently, she reached down and scratched a knee. Again, the twitching rippled through her lower body. Akhila looked down at her legs and smiled. River Father was trying to send her a message.

"No!" she shouted. "I have changed my mind. Let me out here."

Charon stopped rowing.

"What is it, fish girl?"

Akhila turned and marched to the back of the boat. Then she reached out and snatched the beaded necklace from Charon's hand.

"I am not dead!" she shouted. "I have no need for boats or ferrymen. Forgive me, but I will make the journey alone."

Akhila quickly reached up and tied the beads around her neck, marched back to the bow of the boat, then climbed up onto the railing and dove into the Styx.

"Wait!" Charon shouted, rushing to the edge. "Akhila!"

A brilliant silver tale broke the surface of the water

off the port side, then disappeared.

Charon stood staring out at the water for a few minutes. He contemplated going after her, but quickly dismissed the idea. He knew all there was to know about the human spirit. The mermaid would only resist his help. The ferryman looked up at the ash-colored sky and saw a streak of light. Charon shook his head, then plunged the oar back in the water. He turned the boat around and began making his way back to the pier.

"Safe journey, fish girl," he mumbled. "May I never see your star streak the skies above the Styx."

CHAPTER THIRTY-TWO

Hell

Ruki sprinted back through the dark corridor towards the clearing. When he reached the opening, the samurai cautiously leaned out, scoping the space for Nephilim. New pools of blood and flesh debris lay strewn about the floor. Ruki spied two sets of iron shackles that were missing their occupants. As the pools began their slow ascent up the wall, Ruki entered the clearing.

"You," hissed one of the remaining souls.

Ruki inched towards the condemned. "What is it?"

"Why is it you can walk about freely, while I suffer on this wall?" the soul demanded. "Tell me, which of your orifices do you offer up to our captors, that they give you a such special privilege?"

"Bah!" Ruki balked. "I roam freely because I am free. You suffer on that wall because you are condemned. *Jigou jitoku.* Do not compare yourself to me."

The samurai turned on his heel and entered the corridor that made up the west wing of the palace.

"I will see you beside me on this wall!" the soul shouted. "I shall laugh while your stinking guts spill out on the earth, over and OVER!"

Ruki shook his head and picked up the pace.

The shouts and insults from the soul on the wall began to fade, only to be replaced by a sudden outburst of screaming. Two growling voices took turns throwing verbal punches, in between the clatter of unknown objects crashing against the stone walls. Ruki ducted into an open doorway, as the argument spilled out into the corridor.

"Stop hiding the little brat, Uphir,"

"I am hiding nothing, fool!" the physician replied. "The child is gone."

"Liar!"

"I do not have time for your antics, Ba'al. How dare you accuse me!"

"Lucifer will hear of this. I will not be denied a sacrifice from my follower!"

"Your personal whore has no say over the future of that child! Take it up with the general."

"I take nothing up with anyone! If I want the child, I shall have it!"

Ruki's eyes darted back and forth in the blackness, his mind processing the conversation. The child was gone. Which meant Malachi had already found him and stolen him away. Ruki smiled to himself.

"He did it," Ruki mumbled to himself.

"What was that?" Uphir barked.

"A tasty snack," Ba'al replied. "I shall go and see,"

Ruki sucked in a breath as a pair of heavy footsteps came towards the room. The samurai stepped backward into the shadows and drew his katana.

"Come out," Ba'al's voice boomed. "You will pay dearly if I have to come in and fetch you."

The samurai squeezed the handle of his sword, its

leather wraps creaking against his strong fingers.

"What are you waiting for?" Ruki answered, "Come and get me,"

The demon roared and charged into the room, passing right through the samurai, trampling several pieces of furniture and shattering a strange sculpture made of human skulls.

Ruki raised his sword.

"You missed," he whispered, tapping Ba'al on the shoulder.

The demon whipped around.

"What sorcery is this?" he bellowed into the blackened room. "Show yourself! I shall feast on your entrails."

"You will try," Ruki said. His voice bounced and fluttered against the stone walls as if it had a life of its own, brushing past Ba'al like a breeze.

Ba'al swung his meaty fists, swiping at nothing. Enraged, he snatched an iron candelabra from the wall and hurled it across the room, shattering it into a dozen pieces while slopping melted wax on the gray stone floor. As the wax bubbled and smoked, Ba'al paced the room, panting and snarling like a caged animal.

"I will admit, you have the advantage," Ba'al said, panting. "Never have I seen a condemned as strong or as brazen as you. But, we are still your masters,"

He paused, cocking his head to one side.

"Eventually, I am going to win," he continued. "I always win,"

"That is not true," Ruki replied, "and I am not one of your condemned,"

Ba'al took a few more swipes at the darkness. Again,

his fists found nothing but air.

"Why all this cat and mouse?" he bellowed. "If you are not a condemned soul, then why do you hide? Is it because you are a coward? Is it because you know you cannot kill me?"

"Omae wa mou shindeiru," Ruki whispered, stepping into the light coming in from the window.

Ba'al turned and faced the samurai. As his eyes fell on to the katana, a smile spread across his face.

"And what does that mean?" he asked, cracking his knuckles.

Ruki smirked.

"You are already dead."

As the last word left his lips, Ruki lunged, his right leg planting a kick square in the demon's gut.

Ba'al fell backwards, landing with a thud. He leapt to his feet and charged the samurai.

Ruki spun left, rolling himself across Ba'al's back. As he came back around, Ruki slashed the katana's blade across Ba'al's shoulders, flaying them open.

The demon screamed in pain, instinctively reaching behind him.

Again, Ruki swung his blade. This time, the katana cut through Ba'al's wrist, the momentum of the swing severing the big demon's hand from the rest of him.

Ba'al dropped to his knees, scrambling to retrieve his severed hand. His blood, the color and texture of pitch, oozed from his wounds. The corrosive and sticky fluid sizzled and churned, eating away large patches of the floor. He reached under an overturned chair and grabbed his hand. As he started to rise, Ruki quickly planted another kick in his back, forcing Ba'al face down into a bubbling puddle of his own blood.

"Watashi wa anata o hakai shimasu," he hissed through clenched teeth. "I will take your head as my reward."

Ruki raised his sword over his head with both hands. As he brought the katana down, a clawed hand reached in and grabbed him by a wrist, stopping him in mid-swing.

"Who dares—" Ruki barked.

"I dare, samurai," Uphir said, digging his claws into Ruki's flesh. "I cannot allow you to take his head."

Uphir reached up and grasped the katana. As his bare hand wrapped around a portion of the handle, the blade began glow. The bright blue light slowly traveled down into the handle, consuming Ruki's hand and arm.

Uphir and Ba'al both turned away, shielding their eyes from a brightness never seen in the depths of Hell. After several minutes, the light reduced to a low steady glow and when Uphir opened his eyes, he found the katana had become one with its owner.

"The power of Ame-no-Murakumo-no-Tsurugi cannot be contained by one who possesses no valor," Ruki said. "Neither you nor your friend here have any honor. The snake sword knows this."

He tried to pull his arm free of Uphir's grip, but the demon physician held fast.

"Your powers are strong, samurai, but so are mine," Uphir sneered. "Let us see how you fare when your abilities are... shall we say, limited?"

With his free hand, Uphir snapped his fingers, summoning a quintet of dark purple flames at the tips of his claws. The flames flickered, taking on the shape of nude female figures, dancing on the demon's digits. The tiny purple fire figures skipped along the physician's fingers, forming a ring in the palm of his hand. He held his open palm up to his lips and blew out the flames. The smoke from the flames, all thick and gray, hit Ruki square in the face.

The samurai inhaled a mouthful of the smoke and began to cough, forcing the veins in Ruki's temples to bulge and pulse. Sheathing his sword, Ruki dropped to one knee, his hands clutching his throat.

"What... have you... done—"

"Do not be concerned, samurai," Uphir said. "I have not taken anything away from you. But I cannot have you running around killing my brothers."

Ruki staggered to his feet and started for the door.

"If you are able to find a way out of Hell," Uphir continued, "your powers will be restored."

As the samurai stumbled back out into the main corridor of the west wing, Uphir extended a hand to Ba'al.

"That is, *if you find a way,*" he chuckled.

CHAPTER THIRTY-THREE

The air began to cool as Malachi approached the gate. He reached under his tunic and gently caressed the child's soft, fuzzy hair. This child was not Balthazar. Not yet. Malachi tried to remember that. The newborn wiggled and fidgeted beneath his shirt, but had remained completely silent.

The dirt floor crunched under his feet as Malachi approached the gate. The red eyes of Malik's guards loomed all around, their incoherent whispers swirling about in the darkness like specters.

"Make way for the general's son,"

While Malachi strode past, the nineteen silenced their haunting chatter and stood at attention. At the gate stood one lone soldier. Without missing a beat, the demon unlatched the gate and swung it open, allowing Malachi to exit Hell without slowing his pace. When he had cleared the threshold, the gate swung shut.

"Leaving so soon?" Malik muttered.

Malachi turned and found Malik, still in a humanoid form, sitting against the wall.

"I would have thought," he continued, rising to his feet, "that you would want to stay awhile. What, with you being practically royalty and all."

"Careful, Malik," Malachi said, "that stinks of jealousy."

Malik threw his head back and laughed.

"Jealous? Of you?" he roared. "Do not be absurd!"

The demon took a hold of the skin on his chest, then began ripping it away, as if it were a tunic. As the layers of flesh were torn away, once again the hell hound began to emerge from underneath. Malik screamed out in pain as he peeled away the last bits from his backside, revealing that dangerous leathery tail.

"I will hunt the living when lord Lucifer rules the earth," Malik growled. "The open countryside will be my playground. I shall roam free in the light of an eternal full blood moon, feasting off the bones of humans. I am not jealous of your lineage, Malachi. It is but a leash around your neck."

Malachi shook his head.

"So says the dog who stands guard at the gate," he smirked. "Mark my words, you'll never leave this post."

The Sand Dweller turned and began his trek back to Hades.

Chapter Thirty-Four

The Entrance to The Underworld

Akhila followed the river for several miles, occasionally popping her head up out of the water to get her bearings. The shoreline was an endless sprawl of long dead weeds and ancient trails etched into the dry, barren earth. Even the water itself was void of life. Akhila could sense no trace of living creatures, no fish, no monsters, just silent black water creeping into the heart of death.

Then the river cut right, and as she rounded the bend, the entrance of Hades emerged, a great cavernous opening that seemed to devour the very river she traveled. Large ravens dotted the skeletal remains of the trees that book-ended the mouth of the cavern. Akhila eyed them suspiciously, they were the first signs of life she had seen since she had left Charon and his ferry.

As she entered the opening, a shadowy figure stepped out from behind one of the trees, its identity obscured by a hazy mist.

"You there, mermaid," the figure called out. "Are you living or dead?"

Akhila turned and stared at the shadow.

"I am living," she called out.

"Why enter the kingdom of the dead, when you do

not have to?"

Akhila shrugged her shoulders.

"I have business here," she replied. "I was sent by the great spirit of the sea."

The shadow figure didn't reply. It simply vanished back into the haze and dead brush. As quickly as it had come, the mysterious being was gone.

The mermaid continued to coast along, and soon she, like the river Styx was swallowed by the cavern. Her eyes panned up, soaking in every detail of the ceiling, with its dripping stalactites and shimmering texture. Along the edge of the river was a stone path. Cut right into the side of the cavern, the path was smooth and wide, littered with long abandoned artifacts from its many travelers who discovered they could not take it with them.

Up ahead the cavern widened, and Akhila found herself in a sort of harbor. A dock, much like the one she encountered on the open river, sat cold and docile, while ripples of stale water lapped against its stilts. At the end of the dock stood the mysterious shadow figure. Akhila could see the figure much clearer. It appeared to be a man, concealed in a brown riding cloak and derby pulled way down on its face. As she approached the dock, the mysterious figure crouched down and extended a gloved hand.

"Please, let me help you out of the water," it said.

Akhila cocked her head to one side, distrust all over her face. She reached down and grasped a water-logged branch wedged in the silt. Holding it with both hands, the mermaid prepared for the worst.

"Atargatis told me not to trust humans," she said.

Seeing her makeshift weapon, the stranger quickly held his hands up in mock surrender.

"Oh, forgive me," the figure said. It reached up and took off his hat, exposing the bearded face of a handsome Caucasian man. "My name is Donovan. I meet all the newcomers who enter the underworld by way of this river. Although I must say, I have never met a newcomer who was not yet deceased."

Akhila smiled and lowered her weapon, then offered Donovan her hand. With little effort, he pulled Akhila from the water and gently placed her on the dock. The mermaid's tale, now out of the water, immediately split and formed legs. She then stood and faced her new acquaintance.

"I thank you for your assistance," Akhila said. "But I must continue my journey."

She smiled, retrieved her stick and then began to walk towards the clearing that lay beyond the dock.

"Wait!" Donovan warned taking a step towards her. "You mustn't go into the underworld like that,"

Akhila looked back and gave him a puzzled frown.

"Like what?" she asked.

Donovan unbuttoned his cloak and removed it. Then he stepped forward and gently draped it across her shoulders.

"There," he said, fastening the button under her chin. "We cannot have you running around naked."

Akhila felt around under the cloak and found two slits in the sides. She pushed her arms through one at a time, then smoothed the garment around her waist and legs. The fabric was soft and heavy, and smelled of its previous wearer. Akhila glanced up at Donovan and smiled.

"Thank you," she said. "But I am afraid I have nothing to give you in return."

"My lady, you have nothing I require," Donovan replied. "It is my duty to greet and if necessary guide those who have crossed over from the land of the living."

"That must be a great honor," Akhila said. "So many people—"

"Oh, I do not meet everyone who dies," Donovan replied. "There are many others like me, from all cultures. The underworld is full of spirit guides. Tell me, what is your name?"

"I am Akhila, Mermaid of the Flint Place," Akhila answered.

Donovan bowed deeply.

"I am honored to meet you, Akhila. Are you in need of a guide?"

Akhila looked around. Beyond the dock was a large clearing, then three corridors all leading in different directions.

"Where do those lead?" she asked, pointing at the tunnels.

Donovan walked over and stood beside her.

"Those are the underground roads that lead to the different levels of the afterlife,"

"Which one is the underworld my patron would know?" she asked.

Donovan scratched his copper colored beard. "Well, that depends. Who is your patron?"

Akhila grinned proudly.

"My patron is the god of the sea, Poseidon," she

declared. "It is he who sent me on this journey."

"I see," Donovan said with a nod. "Then you should take the far right tunnel. That is the one that leads to the realm of his brother, Hades."

"Hades," Akhila muttered under her breath.

"Yes," Donovan said. "It is the name of the place as well as its ruler."

"But," the mermaid frowned, "how do I get to Orcus?"

Donovan turned and stared at her in shock.

"Are you from Italy, Akhila?" he asked.

Akhila shook her head. "No, I am Akwesasne. My people are from the west. Why do you ask?"

"Well," he replied, "because only a small population of ancient Romans would know the name Orcus. Where did you hear it?"

"In a dream," she said.

"Ah... I see," Donovan sighed, his hand back to scratching his beard. "You had a vision from one of the gods. Or perhaps even *the* God."

"I do not understand," Akhila said.

"You do not have to understand it, just obey," Donovan said. "Come, I will take you to the dwelling of Hades and his queen. Your timing is impeccable. It is said that the Fates arrived in the palace today. They should be able to decipher your vision. The Fates know all there is to know about all there is."

CHAPTER THIRTY-FIVE

The Gates of Hades

As Akhila and her guide stepped out of the tunnel, she was overcome by the size of the large gates that lay before them. Cast in black iron, the large pair of doors were adorned with intricate scenes of life in the world of the living. Akhila ran her hands along the surface of the gate, her finger tips taking in every detail. Her eyes panned down towards the bottom of the gate, to a scene she already knew. A river running into a great cavern, ending at a pair of gates, guarded by a great three headed dog-like creature. Akhila pulled her hand back and shuttered.

"What of this monster?" she asked, pointing to the carving.

"His name is Cerberus," Donovan said. "Gatekeeper of Hades. He is said to be the three headed beast that prevented the dead from leaving the underworld."

"Where is the creature now?" Akhila asked glancing around.

Donovan smiled and gave Akhila a pat on the back. "Cerberus has been gone for many years. Taken, by Heracles and given to Eurystheus, King of Tiryns."

"The Pillar of Heracles," Akhila blurted out.

"Come again?" Donovan said.

"I have been to the Pillar of Heracles," Akhila said. "Is this the same man?"

Donovan chuckled and took a hold of the left gate. With one good shove, the heavy iron door swung open. Then he turned and beckoned the mermaid forward.

"Well, come on," he said.

Akhila passed through the gateway into a large open foyer. She noticed right away the stillness of the air and lack of sounds. To her right was a short path that led straight into a large wall. To the left was a seemingly well walked and dark path, adorned with high archways and the occasional statue.

She took a few steps towards the large jagged wall.

"Why does that path lead to a wall with no gate?" she asked.

"Oh, there is a gate," Donovan said. "That wall is the entrance for your mysterious Orcus."

Akhila's face lit up. "Really? Can we go through it?"

The guide shook his head.

"No," he said, "It would take you back to the surface, to the land of the living. To see Orcus, you will need to travel the arched path."

The two set off on the left path, and were soon consumed by the gloom that filled the dimly lit trail. Donovan did his best to regale the mermaid with the stories behind the many marble and granite statues that cropped up along the way. Akhila soaked it all in, her imagination flooded with tales of golden apples, giant sea monsters and vamps whose eyes could turn mortal men to stone with just a glance. Her thoughts returned to her little sister back home. Akhila couldn't wait to get back to her tribe and retell these stories to the children.

Up ahead, the glow of blue light broke through the darkness. A sudden burst of crisp spring air flooded the path, its chill raising the hairs on Akhila's arms and neck.

"We are close now," Donovan said.

As they approached the entrance to the throne room, a pair of voices, deep in conversation drifted out with the breeze.

"Hades, one of my servants just informed me that the Moirai have arrived. Where is the Sand Dweller and the Samurai?"

"Patience my dear," Hades replied. "He only just arrived a moment ago. As soon as he gets the child situated and tidy's himself up, they will all meet us here."

"This plan must work, Hades. I cannot bare another century here."

Hades sighed heavily. "My dear, you must trust me. The only force strong enough to overthrow Zeus is from Heaven, and this child is the key to that power. We will raise up a warrior so fierce that even that fool Heracles will shudder in fear."

"Yes but what of Malachi? He is not just going to let you take his child—"

"To Hell with Malachi!" bellowed Hades.

The rage in Hade's voice gave Akhila a shutter. She turned to Donovan, her eyes pleading with him.

"What is it?" Donovan whispered.

"Who is this god?" she whispered back.

"Hades," Donovan replied. "The ruler over Hades and Orcus."

"He is planning something terrible for this Sand

Dweller," she said. "I must help him if I can."

Donovan slowly started backing away from the mermaid.

"Where are you going?" she whispered, reaching out a hand. "Are you not going to help me?"

"You are mad, if you think I want any part of interfering in the affairs of Hades." he answered. "I am sorry Akhila, but you are on your own from here."

New voices funneled out from the throne room. Akhila cocked her head, listening to see who the new arrivals were.

"Ah, there you are, Hades,"

"Welcome ladies," Hades responded. "It has been too long."

"We are anxious to see the soulless child. When will it be arriving?"

"At any moment," Hades said. "Soon, we will shake the powers of Olympus to its foundations. Poseidon and Zeus will finally pay for leaving me down here to rot amongst the dead."

At mention of her patron's name, Akhila's eyes grew narrow with anger. Her heart suddenly understood why she had been bound to the River Father, why she had studied under Atargatis and why the black current had brought her to the underworld. The child. She needed to rescue the child. Akhila looked back down the darkened path. It was empty. Donovan was gone.

Akhila took a deep breath and turned her attention back to the conversation in the throne room. She would learn all she could, and when the time was right, she would make her move.

CHAPTER THIRTY-SIX

Mount Olympus

Zeus stood at the edge of the open terrace gazing out at the horizon, his arm draped around a nearby column as if it were a secret lover. He closed his eyes and breathed deep. The air at the top of his mountain was sweet and crisp, especially in the morning. Opening his eyes, Zeus watched lazy clouds pass by, casting cool shadows on the face of Mount Olympus. Morning was his favorite time. It was only in the morning hours that he could reflect on all he had seen and done, without intrigue and regret worming its way in.

"We need to talk, little eaglet,"

The god of thunder and lightning winced. It had been a long time since anyone had called him that. No one on Olympus or in the human world would dare to be so informal. A pet name given to him as a child, *little eaglet* was a monicker the Greek god wished would disappear. Within the seemingly harmless name, the truth of his lineage hid like a thief, waiting to unmask the truth of his bloodline.

There was only one who kept the demeaning title alive.

"Greetings, Gabriel," Zeus replied, turning around. "How is my favorite uncle?"

Gabriel snorted.

"I thought Michael was your favorite,"

"My favorite is always the one who comes to call on me," Zeus said with a sigh, "since I cannot venture up to visit any of you. As you can see, I am right where *He* left me."

"You are too old to be pouting," Gabriel replied, rolling his eyes, "and I am not here for a social call, so spare me your endless lamenting."

Zeus clasped his hands behind his back and slowly began pacing back and forth in front of Gabriel.

"Very well uncle," Zeus said, staring at the floor as he strolled back and forth. "What is it you wish to speak to me about?"

"In a few days time, members of the Heavenly Host will be bringing a guest here," Gabriel began.

"What do you mean, a guest?" Zeus asked.

"A newborn child," Gabriel continued, "a boy, will be brought here and is to remain here as your guest and protege until The Most High sends for him,"

"A baby?" Zeus scoffed.

"Yes,"

"Here?" Zeus growled.

"Yes,"

The son of Chronos threw his hands up in disgust.

"Absolutely not!" he barked.

Gabriel's wings shot out from under his armor, and in a split second, the Archangel was in the air. Then he swooped down, grabbing Zeus by the neck and with one arm, lifted him up off the ground.

"Listen to me, Nephilim," Gabriel commanded. "This is not a request, it is an order! You *will* keep the child here, you *will* keep him safe and you *will* teach him everything that is possible to teach him. Do you understand?"

Gabriel let go of Zeus's neck and watched him fall to the floor.

"Why must the child come here?" Zeus said, stumbling to his feet. "Who will be looking for him, that The Most High would hide him here?"

The angel glided over to the open end of the terrace and set down on the ledge.

"There are many," Gabriel said. "All of whom are either too ignorant or too fearful to come looking for him on Olympus."

Zeus raised an eyebrow.

"Who is this child?" he asked.

"For now all you need know is that he is your extended family and you will treat him as such."

"And?" Zeus asked.

Gabriel cocked his head to one side.

"And what?"

"*And,*" Zeus replied, "what is in it for me to house my dear little cousin?"

Gabriel shook his head and stepped off the ledge of the terrace. His massive wings pumped slowly, keeping the Archangel hovering in the air.

"You have received all that you would ever receive a long time ago, little eaglet," Gabriel answered. "You six Olympians were spared from the wrath that befell the other Nephilim. Never forget that you owe him."

The Archangel glided out away from the terrace and disappeared in to the morning clouds.

CHAPTER THIRTY-SEVEN

The Throne Room of Hades

"Clotho, Lachesis, Atropos," Hades said, opening his arms wide to the sisters, "You remember my queen, Persephone?"

Persephone bowed her head and dropped into her best curtsy. She knew better than to show the Fates anything but her utmost respect. It was common knowledge that all gods, save one, could not help but bend to the will of the Moirai. They controlled the mother thread of life, and could disconnect the lifeline of any lesser god at will.

The three Fates glided across the marble floor and swirled around Persephone. Their white robes flowing in air like petals on a breeze.

"It is a pleasure to see you again, my dear," Clotho said.

"Yes," the other two said in unison, "we are grateful for your hospitality,"

The Fates broke apart then returned to Hades.

"Your note was most intriguing, Hades," Atropos whispered.

Lachesis nodded in agreement. "We wondered what was going to become of the empty child,"

"But when we received word from you," Clotho

chimed in, "we knew instantly what to do."

Two servants entered the throne room carrying a waist high altar, followed by two more servants each holding a woven basket, shrouded by pieces of blue linen.

"Ah, good," Hades called out, "place it all here in the center."

The servants immediately got to work, dressing the long marble alter. They quickly arranged the linens, candles and the like, carefully placing each item around the outer edges of the altar. In the center, a small, oblong cushion was placed, complete with branches of laurel, a crust of bread and a chalice filled with wine. When the servants had finished, they lined up in front of the altar, heads down, and waited to be dismissed.

The three Fates drifted towards the completed display and began to circle it, muttering under their breath, while adjusting the positions of a few stray items. Satisfied with the finished altar, they floated back and faced the servants.

"You have all done very well," they said in unison.

Hades snapped his fingers and pointed to the door.

"You may go now," he commanded.

As the servants filed out of the throne room, Malachi entered, his arms cradling the stoic newborn child of him and Zilpah. He strode across the room, stopping short of the three floating women who seemed all too eager to see the bundle he was carrying.

"He has arrived," Clotho whispered, edging towards Malachi.

"And he has brought the child," the other Fates continued.

Within seconds, Malachi and the child were

surrounded by the Fates. He stood motionless and tense for a few moments, while the weavers of destiny cooed and caressed the child.

"It is not often that we get the privilege of seeing the empty shell," Lachesis said.

Atropos nodded. "Or the finished specimen. This will be a special day, indeed."

Clotho leaned down, her face inches from the child. She studied the expressionless baby a moment, then glanced up at Malachi and smiled.

"He will have the look of his father," she whispered. "I promise you,"

Hades took Persephone by the hand and led her to Malachi and the child.

"Young Sand Dweller," he said, "allow me to present my wife, Persephone, the Queen of Hades."

Malachi offered a single nod. "It is my pleasure, your Majesty,"

Hades gave a quick glance over Malachi's shoulder.

"Where is your guide?" he asked. "I expected you and Ruki to attend this ritual."

"He has not yet returned," Malachi answered. "I hope nothing has happened to him."

Persephone giggled.

"My dear boy," she said, "Ruki is a spirit guide. He has already experienced death and was granted great honors by the powerful, Izanami no Mikoto for his heroics in life. Nothing can happen to him."

"Besides," Hades injected, "he may have just returned to his regular duties. You are not his only job here."

Malachi smiled and let out a sigh.

"You are right," he said. "I should not aspire to keep all of his attention to myself."

Clotho broke away from the group and began to flutter back to the altar.

"There is no need to delay the ritual any longer," she said, positioning herself behind the altar.

Lachesis and Atropos soon joined her, taking their place on either side of their sister. Clotho stretched out her hand and beckoned Malachi forward.

"Bring the vessel here, young Sand Dweller," she said.

Malachi strode forward, shifting the child in his arms as he approached the altar. With both hands, he carefully handed the child across the altar to Clotho, then stood back.

"No, no," Lachesis and Atropos called out. "Do not step away. We will need some of your thread, Malachi Ben Sinai,"

Clotho motioned for Malachi to stand beside her.

"Give me the defixio," she said.

Malachi reached behind his neck and untied the leather cord. Then he handed over the worn rolled piece of lead. His heart jumped in his chest. The prospect of being reunited with Balthazar stirred in his chest. Malachi took a deep breath, expanding his lungs to capacity.

"You have nothing to fear," Clotho muttered. "You are seeing what no humans ever see. Relish in this opportunity, young Sand Dweller. As an immortal, you are privy to all of the secret ways."

Then she removed the curse tablet from its cord and set it down on the altar. With skill, Clotho feverishly waved her hands over the rolled piece of lead, reciting an ancient spell. Soon, Balthazar's soul, glowing bright and green, began to drift up out of the defixio. When the last bit had exited, the green fog hovered in front of Clotho, as if awaiting instructions.

"Open your mouth, Malachi," Clotho said. "I need some of your thread."

Malachi hesitated, then slowly opened his mouth. With long, delicate fingers, the Fate reached in and pulled out a length of silver thread, no finer than a single hair.

"This is a piece of the thread that makes up your life," she said, holding the thread up for him to see. "All that you were, all that you are and all that you are destined to be is contained in its weave."

Malachi mouth remained agape, as he stared at the glimmering cord held in front of him.

"We shall entwine your thread, with Balthazar's thread," Lachesis said, "forever binding your lives."

"No matter where you are, or when you are," Atropos added, "your fate's will be linked."

Then the three Moirai plunged a hand into the hovering soul, each pulling out a piece of silver thread.

"I allot this soul all the time needed to fulfill his destiny," Lachesis cried out.

"This soul shall not expire before its time," Atropos said.

Clotho took the ends of the threads from her sisters, then combined them with the two she already had. With expert hands, she tied the ends together and laid the unwoven lengths down on the altar. She then reached into her flowing sleeve, and retrieved a brightly glowing ball of silver life thread.

"This," she declared, holding up the ball, "is the Mother Thread of Life. Its threads bind you to a living existence, and all that comes with it."

She pulled out a thread from the ball, added it to the lengths on the altar, then stashed the ball back in her sleeve. For several minutes the throne room was silent, as Clotho the Spinner weaved all the threads together, tied them off, then cut them into two equal lengths. When she finished, she held them up for all to see.

"Behold," the Fates chimed. "The threads are complete."

Lachesis took one of the newly woven threads and inserted it back into the awaiting soul.

"Go now," she commanded, "I allot you this new vessel to dwell in until you reach the end of your thread."

The glowing soul, like a cloud on the wind, began to creep along the altar. When it located the child's face, it slowly funneled itself into the mouth and nostrils. When the last of the soul had entered the body, the baby's eyes burst open, the telltale signs of consciousness shining through for the first time. Then, as with all newborns, baby Balthazar began to squirm and cry.

Malachi's lungs deflated as relief washed over his brow. With a shaky hand, he reached down and caressed the baby's soft spot.

"It is good to have you back, my brother," he said. "I have missed your face."

Clotho placed her pale hand on Malachi's shoulder. He turned and saw her other hand held the now empty defixio, dangling from the second piece of newly woven life thread. With both hands, she gently wrapped it around his neck and sealed the two ends at the back.

"This binds you two in spirit and destiny for all time," she said. "It can never be removed, and only Atropos or The Most High *Himself* can break it."

Tears welled in the corners of Malachi's eyes.

"There is nothing I can offer you that will express how grateful I am," Malachi began.

"We have done nothing special," Lachesis said, "Our whole existence centers around the threads,"

The other Moirai nodded in agreement.

Hades and Persephone glanced at one another and smiled. Only one loose end needed to be tied.

"This is a most joyous occasion," Hades proclaimed, clapping his hands. Walking to the wall, he yanked on a tasseled cord.

Instantly a pair of servant souls entered.

"We need food and drink!" Hades barked. "Tonight we celebrate birth in the realm of the dead!"

Clotho grabbed up the forgotten piece of bread, ripped out a small piece from the center and dipped it into the wine chalice. The other two Fates casually drifted away from the altar, their gaze never leaving the Sand Dweller.

"There is no reason why the young Balthazar should not celebrate with us," Clotho declared, shaking the excess drips of wine off of the soaked bread. Her cold stare rose to meet Hade's. "Right?"

As the Moirai reached over to place the wine-soaked bread into the baby's mouth, Malachi's hand shot out and slapped the food away.

"No, fool!" Malachi screamed. "Are you mad?"

Chapter Thirty-Eight

Hell

Ba'al released a roar from the pit of his guts.

"Stop moving, imbecile!" Uphir barked, slapping the demon across the back of the head.

"The pain," Ba'al hissed, "I cannot take the pain!"

Uphir threw his head back and laughed, then jammed the needle back into the open wound on Ba'al's shoulder.

"Stop your foolish grumbling! This wound must be sewn up," Uphir replied, pulling the length of thread through, "It will never heal, but at least it will not fester. Much."

Ba'al shook his head and grabbed a hold of the table in front of him. Not since the fall had he felt real pain. The wounds reminded him of the ones he received fighting the angels. His only remaining hand dug into stone table top as Uphir once again plunged the needle into his back.

"I do not understand," Ba'al said, "only an Archangel's sword should have been capable of these kinds of injuries. Will they heal?"

Uphir shrugged his shoulders. "I do not think so, brother."

Ba'al looked down at his leather wrapped stump then cast a worried glance over his shoulder. "What of my hand?" he asked.

"There is nothing I can do about that now," the physician replied with a smirk. "Perhaps in the future you will keep your appendages out of the way in a fight."

"You bastard!" Ba'al raged, swinging his fist around behind him.

Uphir stepped back, easily avoiding the swing. Then he reached out and grabbed a handful of Ba'al's wound. The big demon's corrosive blood bubbled out between the physician's fingers as he squeezed.

Ba'al lurched forward, screaming in pain.

"Now, you listen to me," Uphir snarled, "You want your hand restored? Then you are going to do something for me."

A blast of angry sulfur blasted from Ba'al's nostrils.

"Name it," he grumbled.

"Azazael's son took the child into Hades," Uphir said. "Retrieve the child and bring him to me."

"What if I decide I want the child for myself?" Ba'al asked with a smirk.

Uphir chuckled. "My only interest is in the soul of the child. The soul of the little immortal,"

Ba'al jerked away from Uphir's grasp and stood.

"And what of the rest?"

"The rest," Uphir replied, "is yours to do with as you wish,"

"Why do you only want the soul of the immortal?" Ba'al asked.

"Because he owes me for a service I did him," Uphir said, "and I always get paid for my services."

Ba'al started for the door.

"Consider it done, brother," he said.

As Ba'al stormed out the door, Uphir got to the business of gathering up and putting away his instruments. He never dreamed he would come face to face with the opportunity to obtain a soul that had yet to be judged. The demon physician's mouth watered at the prospect. So many experiments he had always wanted to conduct.

"Surely Heaven will not miss one, measly soul," he muttered to himself.

"Who's soul?" Zilpah asked, stepping into the room. "Where is my child?"

Uphir's shoulders rocked as he chuckled.

"I have sent Ba'al to fetch him," Uphir answered. "It would seem the general's son crept into Hell and stole the little beast away."

Zilpah hissed, baring her fangs.

"You did this!" she growled, "You lost my son!"

She broke into a run, slamming into the demon with both hands. Tears evaporated from the corners of her eyes as over and over she beat her fists against Uphirs chest.

Calmly the physician took a hold of Zilpha's wrists and in one fluid motion, flung her to the floor.

"I think it is most amusing," Uphir sneered, "anytime a half breed imposter comes down into my domain and *pretends* to be a real demon."

The physician sighed and casually brushed his robes with the back of his hands.

"At the end of the day," he continued, "you are just a worthless copycat, playing games you cannot possibly master."

As he took a step towards her, Zilpah scooted backwards.

"Oh, no, no, no," Uphir said, snatching her up by the front of her bedclothes. "You are not at liberty to run away from me."

Uphir pulled her face close to his and grinned, brandishing his own set of deadly canines.

"You see," he said, "after I extract the little immortal's soul from the child, I have no doubt that your all mighty Ba'al will eat the remains—"

"NO!" Zilpah cried, trying to pull away.

"But," Uphir continued, "now that I know children can be sired down here in Hell and that souls can placed inside them—"

Zilpah struggled harder.

"Wait, what do you mean?" she whimpered through clenched teeth.

"Oh yes," Uphir replied. "Did you think your pregnancy was the result of a night of passion? The half breed used you. He needed a vessel for the little immortal. For his precious Balthazar."

Zilpah's eyes narrowed as the truth settled in her mind. She had thought about the night she spent with Malachi every day for nine months. Fantasized about the life they could live, just the three of them.

Uphir gingerly released his hold on her and stepped back.

"It has always been about the human," she said.

"Yes it has," Uphir said.

"I will never have Malachi to myself until that human

is out of the way." she said.

"That is why you will go back to your chambers and let me take care of this mess," Uphir said. "I will call for you if I need you."

Zilpah staggered out into the corridor and pulled the door shut behind her. As she started down the path towards her chambers, more tears welled up in her eyes. She knew if she followed Uphir's instructions, she would never be free of his control.

"I will be no one's baby farm," she muttered.

As the door to her chambers came into view, Zilpah decided it was now or never. She quickened her pace, bypassing her rooms and continuing down the long, dark corridor that led to the gates.

CHAPTER THIRTY-NINE

Malachi snatched the baby from the altar and backed up towards the door.

"Do you know what you could have done?" he bellowed.

"Yes, I do," Clotho answered. "And I am happy to see that you stopped me."

Malachi pressed the child against his chest.

"I do not understand," he said. "What is going on here?"

"We had to be sure you truly had Balthazar's best interests at heart," Lachesis said.

"That you would protect him," Atropos chimed in.

The Moirai drifted out from behind the altar and quickly surrounded the Sand Dweller. Their white linens swayed and fluttered on the still air, slowly brightening from a light coming off of their skin.

"Bless you, Malachi Ben Sinai," the three Fates whispered. "Yours is a destiny fit for a hero. Now, take the Orcus Child and go!"

"Thank you," Malachi replied.

He turned and briskly marched towards the door.

Enraged, Persephone ripped at Hade's robes.

"Stop him!" she cried. "Do not let him take the child!"

Hades stood stoic as a wave of somber emotion washed over his whole body. He gazed down into the frantic eyes of his beloved and shook his head.

"I cannot," he said, brushing a stray piece of hair from her face. "We took a gamble and we lost. The Moirai have given him their blessing. We must not interfere."

"You did this," Persephone yelled, pointing a shaky finger at the three Fates. "We had a deal!"

"Yes, we did," the Fates said. "But we cannot inject our own desires into a being whose destiny has been written by The Most High."

Persephone yanked a dagger from the folds of her gown and started for the door.

"Maybe you lack the courage, but I do not," she spat.

Atropos reached into her sleeve and pulled out a long silver thread. She took a hold of each of the ends and gently tugged, until the life thread was taut.

A pain ripped through Persephone, starting in her head, then vibrating down into her knees. She stopped dead in her tracks, clutching her temples.

"How dare you attempt to inject your will upon that which is inevitable," Atropos voice boomed.

"Arrg..., let me go!" Persephone pleaded.

Atropos yanked on the thread, sending another shock wave of pain through the queen's body.

"You do not control fate, your highness," Atropos said, "We do."

The Moirai let go of one end of the thread. As the end of thread drooped down towards the floor, Persephone followed suit. She lay there a moment, catching her breath while the pain in her head and legs subsided. Then she rolled over into the fetal position and began to sob.

***

Malachi broke into a steady jog, retracing his steps towards the wall of Orcus. He looked down at Balthazar's face and smiled. The baby remained quiet, in spite of his purple, newborn cheeks jiggling from the pace.

He had left so quickly, Malachi didn't see Akhila lurking outside the throne room. As his thoughts mulled over travel plans and the prospect of raising a child, he didn't notice her following him out of Hades either.

The mermaid stayed close to the walls, careful to keep hidden in the shadows that stretched out from the various statues that lined the road. Still gripping the stick she pulled from the river, Akhila maintained a short distance behind the Sand Dweller.

As Malachi approached the crossroads of The Orcus Wall and the gates of Hades, the pounding in his chest began to ease. He held Balthazar close to his chest.

"We are almost home, brother," he whispered.

He reached the end of the arched tunnel, then froze. The stillness and scentless air had changed. In their place was a foreign warmth, coupled with the telltale odor of sulfur. Cautiously, Malachi peeked out into open and was greeted by a fist to the face.

Malachi stumbled back into the arched tunnel, losing his grip on Balthazar. The child landed near a crumbling statue of Hermes and immediately began to cry.

"You have something that belongs to me," Ba'al

growled.

The big demon snatched Malachi by the ankle and dragged him into the open.

"First, you need to be taught a lesson," Ba'al said, picking Malachi up by his tunic. "Did no one teach you? It is a sin to steal..."

With all his strength, Ba'al rammed Malachi against the wall.

Malachi coughed and groaned.

"What do you want?" he stuttered.

Ba'al reared back and slammed him into the wall again.

"The child," he snarled, "I want the child."

As the words left his foul lips, Ba'al flung Malachi to the ground. He laid there a moment, anger and reason swirling in his head. A black presence emerged from deep in the back of his mind, one he had not felt in many years. Images began to flash in his eyes. He saw his demon self, the part Malachi had been desperately trying to keep in check for well over a thousand years.

"Go ahead," Ba'al egged on, "Let it come,"

Malachi struggled to his knees as the demon within took over. His fiery wings shot out from his back, scorching his tunic to ash and blackening the walls. As his skin strained against his body, Malachi's eyes washed over with a glowing red hue. Now standing taller than the mighty Ba'al, Malachi stepped forward and released an ear-splitting roar.

Hidden by the darkness of the tunnel, Akhila watched, horrified by Malachi's transformation. She looked down at the foot of the statue of Hermes and saw little Balthazar. Crouching down, she pulled back his bindings and checked him for injuries.

"I cannot leave you here for those monsters," she whispered, looking around. "Perhaps—"

Quickly, Akhila stripped the baby down to his simple cloth diaper and set him aside. Then she grabbed her stick from the river. Holding it in her hand, Akhila was suddenly struck with the answer. She snapped the stick into two arm length pieces, then concealed them in Balthazar's wraps. As the wood made contact with the warmth left behind by the baby's body, it began to soften and change, forming the exact shape and look of the child that once occupied the cloth.

Akhila exhaled and stumbled backwards. With a hesitant hand, she reached out and touched the changeling's tiny palm. Instinctively, it took a hold her finger and squeezed. She smiled at her creation and pulled her finger away.

"Oh great patron," she whispered under her breath, "you have blessed me with the perfect decoy."

Akhila stood up, stripped off Donovan's brown cloak and tossed it aside near the changeling.

"Come little one," she said, "I will save you from these devils."

Then, she scooped up Balthazar and inched out into the crossroads, carefully keeping herself pressed against the wall as she made her way to the tunnel leading to the Styx.

CHAPTER FORTY

Malachi swiped a sinewy clawed hand, slashing Ba'al across the face. As the big demon stumbled backwards, he swiped again, this time ripping through Ba'al's chest.

Ba'al howled and stumbled back.

"Your powers are strong, son of Azazael," Ba'al gasped. "Why waste them defending a worthless child?"

Demon Malachi pumped his fervid wings, their hot winds throwing dust and gravel in Ba'al's face. As he lifted himself off the ground, Malachi pointed an accusing finger at him.

"You are Ba'al."

Ba'al shrugged, wiping a streak of blood from the corner of his mouth.

"What of it, boy?" he replied, shielding his eyes with his stumped arm.

"Zilpah once told me I would see you in Hell," Malachi growled. "She said you would make me a king. Ruler of all the world."

A grin crept across Ba'al's face.

"She was right," he said, "I can do that."

"If that is true," Malachi asked, "then why are you here, lurking in realms not your own, trying to kidnap helpless babies?"

Before Ba'al could answer, Malachi lunged, plunging

his long, clawed fingers into Ba'al's chest and pressing him against the wall. The big demon twisted and lurched, trying in vain to escape, while Malachi's talons latched on to a pair of ribs.

"You have no real power," Malachi growled through clenched teeth. "You are just a pathetic has been, desperately clinging to authority you no longer have."

With a grunt, Malachi ripped the pair of ribs from Ba'al's chest, then sank them into his shoulders, tacking him to the wall. Then in one final act of insult, Malachi took one last swipe, opening Ba'al's throat.

Ba'al slumped forward, his blood flowing down the front of him like a cascade of acid. His eyes slowly clouded over, changing from an empty black, to a fuzzy gray.

"It is not over," Ba'al's voice gurgled, "I will see you again,"

As the last word escaped his lips, the demon once called the first king of Hell fell into unconsciousness.

Malachi dropped to the ground. While his fiery wings dissipated, he could feel the demon inside him slowly retreat back into the recesses of his mind. Within a few moments, his human body was restored. He wiped the dirt and sweat from his face, then remembering Balthazar, began scanning the ground. As his eyes fell on a pile of cloth just inside the archway, a wave of relief washed over him.

"There you are," he said, stumbling over to the child.

He picked up the brown cloak that lay next to the baby and frowned. His eyes quickly scanned the corridor.

"Is someone there?" he called out.

Malachi looked down at the remains of his scorched tunic and sighed. Without unbuttoning the cloak, he pulled the whole garment over his head.

"At least I have something to cover up with," he said, gathering up the baby. "Come on brother, we have overstayed our welcome in the underworld."

On wobbly legs, the Sand Dweller walked to the end of clearing. He stood there a moment, staring at the large wall that had brought him to the realm of the dead so many months ago. His thoughts wandered as he relived the moment he met Ruki. Malachi's heart grew heavy as he wondered what had become of his new friend. Quickly he shook off the worry and began pressing his palm into the stone, searching for the portal.

"Ah, here it is," he said, pressing his hand through the wall, just as he had on the first day.

"Malachi, stop! Do not leave me!"

He turned around and saw Zilpah running towards him. He pressed Balthazar close to his chest and waited.

"You were just going to go?" she said, panting. "After all we have shared? After creating a child?"

"What *we* have shared?" Malachi laughed. "Tell me, can you even remember all the things you have done to destroy me?"

Zilpah shook her head and took a step forward. "That was in the past—"

"It will never be just in the past!" Malachi fired back. "You murdered my closest friend. You murdered that poor girl in Venice, just to get to me. Everyone you touch turns to ash and death, Zilpah."

"No," she cried, "That is not true—"

"Yes it is," Malachi said. "I only came here to right the wrong you did to Balthazar. I have my friend back, so now I am leaving."

Zilpah reached out with a shaky hand.

"Please stay," she mumbled through her tears. "I love you. You are more to me than just a conquest now."

"Perhaps," he replied, stepping backward through the wall. "But my heart is not willing to take that chance. I am sorry."

His last image of the underworld would be Zilpah running towards the wall.

The forgotten scent of damp stone and moss filled his nostrils. Safely back inside the mouth of the Ogre, Malachi let out a deep sigh of relief. It had been a long nine months. As he strode over and sat down at the stone table in the center of the room, his mind drifted back to what Ruki had said about time having its own rules in the underworld.

"I wonder how long we have actually been gone, my brother," he said pulling back the child's wraps.

His veins flooded with adrenaline as he looked down at the linens. There, where a newborn Balthazar should have been, were a pair of waterlogged sticks.

"NO!" he bellowed. "That bastard will not get away with this!"

Malachi flung the whole lot down on the floor and lurched up out of his seat.

Confidently he marched back to the wall and began to feel around for the opening. Back and forth he walked along the wall, his hand pressing into every inch of stone he could reach. After ten minutes, Malachi gave up. He slumped down on the floor of the cave, his back pressed against the wall, his face streaming with tears. Once again, Balthazar was gone.

CHAPTER FORTY-ONE

Heaven

"I have to tell you, it broke my heart to see young Malachi looking so defeated in the Ogre," lamented Sandalphon, "sitting on that damp floor, sobbing into his hands...it is moments like that one that make me love humans the most."

Gabriel filled a chalice with ambrosia and set down in front of Sandalphon, before plopping himself down in a chair beside him.

"You are a good comfort to suffering men," he replied, pouring himself a cup. "And I am certain you will find a way to ease his burden."

Sandalphon nodded and took a drink from his cup.

"Yes, I will," he said. "And ultimately, he will be filled with great joy. But I understand how each of them feel when it appears that life has turned its back on them."

He paused and took another sip from his cup. "Did you talk to Zeus?"

Gabriel rolled his eyes.

"Oh yes," he said with a smirk.

"How did he take the news?"

"Our little eaglet is most unhappy about his house guest," Gabriel snorted. "But he will comply. He knows he has no choice."

"Good," Sandalphon said, smiling, "I cannot wait to see Malachi's face when they are reunited. I know it is centuries from now, but I am excited, just the same."

The guardian angel pushed his chair back and stood up. Then he emptied his chalice in one gulp.

Until then, I have countless others who need me."

"So now what?" Gabriel asked, rising from his own seat.

"Now we wait," Sandalphon replied. "There are still a great many things that need to happen before they meet again. We two have done our part. All that remains is for Baracheil and Nuriel to deliver the child to Olympus. After that, we report for our next assignment."

CHAPTER FORTY-TWO

November 22nd, 1593, The Mohawk River

The sun bounced off the water, sending pale blue reflections of light up into Akhila's face. She and the child had reached the Mohawk River in record time, and none too soon. The call of the salmon spawn had begun shortly after they had exited the Styx, growing in intensity with each day she spent on the open ocean. The need to swim up the river of her birthplace put pressure on every fiber of her being. When she and Balthazar finally reached their destination, Akhila could feel the weight slough off like dead scales.

She lifted the child up from under his arms so his head and chest were above the current.

"See there, winged one," Akhila said, nodding towards a path that led from the river's edge into the forest. "That is the trail to my people. Your new home."

Balthazar offered a gummy grin, then swayed his head around and planted his face into Akhila's chest. He had been born just a month before, but already was showing signs of being an old soul.

Akhila laughed out loud and gave the baby a tender squeeze.

"Yes, winged one," she chuckled. "I think they will love you too."

She dog paddled to the edge of the river, then willed her fins to split into human legs. As she stepped out of the water, Akhila glanced over at a large rock near the path and squealed with delight.

A neatly folded pile of clothes lay on top of the rock, along with small basket of blue berries and a pair of shoes.

"You see?" Akhila said walking to the rock, "They are expecting us."

The mermaid quickly dressed, then greedily gobbled down the pile of berries. The supplies were all setting on a soft piece of tanned suede. Leaving none of the provisions to waste, Akhila lovingly wrapped Balthazar in the skin.

"There you go," she said, gathering the baby up in her arms. "Now you are ready to meet your new family."

Akhila set out on the trail. As she walked along the dirt path, she breathed in deep, taking in the scent of the sycamores and pines that spread out for miles in all directions. The voices of large ravens echoed through the trees, while countless song birds and crickets chirped closer to the forest floor.

Up ahead, trails of smoke weaved up into the sky. Her nostrils filled with the scents of roasting meat, enticing Akhila's feet to pick up pace.

"Akhila!" a child announced from one of the trees, "Akhila has returned!"

As she entered the clearing of long houses, Akhila found herself surrounded by dozens of smiling, familiar faces. A pair of arms wrapped themselves around her leg. Looking down, she saw her little sister, now a head taller, smiling up at her. Akhila laughed as she stroked the girl's long hair.

"Hello little sister," she said, giving the child a squeeze.

"Akhila, I missed you," the little girl replied.

"Is that my daughter?"

Akhila looked up and saw Bonsari wading through the crowd, a half full basket of blue berries balanced on her hip. She stopped a few feet away and pointed with her free hand at Balthazar.

"What is that?" Bonsari exclaimed. "Is that a child? Akhila, where did you get a child?"

As Bonsari approached, murmurs began to vibrate out from the crowd. She sat down her basket, then reached out and took Balthazar from Akhila.

"Let me see this child," she said.

Bonsari pulled back the skin and began to inspect the baby.

"I see it is a son," she mumbled. Then she flipped Balthazar over and let out a screech.

"Please, let me explain," Akhila began.

Other women elders from the tribe crowded in for a closer look.

"Akhila," Bonsari stuttered, "this child has wings."

"Yes, I know," Akhila replied. "He is not a man. He is something else."

"Is he yours?" Bonsari asked, glaring at Akhila, "Are you his mother?"

Akhila shook her head.

"No, I saved him from monsters in the land of the dead."

More gasps came from the crowd as Bonsari wrapped Balthazar back in the skin and handed him off to another elder. Then she held out her arms and smiled at Akhila.

"My daughter, I believe you."

Akhila ran into her mother's embrace and crushed herself against her. Her cheeks taking in the familiar feel of her mother's bosom, while her hands clung to the familiar softness of her mother's waist. She inhaled deeply. In the arms of her mother, Akhila was home.

"Akhila," Bonsari said, pulling away, "Your father should be back from the hunt this afternoon. But, there is someone else already here who would be very happy to see you again."

Bonsari nudged her daughter, then pointed behind her.

Akhila glanced over her shoulder. There at the back of the crowd was Tsio, his eyes full of hope, as he swayed back and forth in an attempt to get a better view. As their eyes met, a relieved smile spread across his face. Then he broke into a run, closing the distance between them in a matter of seconds.

Akhila felt her heart swell with love as Tsio scooped her up and pressed his lips against hers. She closed her eyes and leaned into the kiss. The fire in his heart had indeed brought her home.

That night, Akhila regaled the tribe with the story of how she came to acquire a non-human child. Surrounded by wide eyes and silent stares, she told them of Charon and the river of the dead, the endless caverns and the many corridors that led the dead to their underworld.

When she spoke of the battle between Malachi and Ba'al, the children squealed and the men leaned forward in their seats, eager to hear all of the bloody details.

"It was during the battle that I found this child," Akhila said, rocking a sleepy Balthazar in her lap, while she herself sat nestled in the arms of Tsio. "I could not leave this baby in the hands of monsters, so I held him close to me and we made our escape."

Heads nodded in agreement around the community fire. Akhila had done the right thing.

"I did not know what to do with him," she continued, "but I knew he would be safe and loved here."

"Akhila, could he be a child of the thunders?"

From the blackness of the woods, Oka'ra softly entered the clearing and stood in the center beside the fire.

"I—" Akhila paused. "I do not know. I never saw any thunders while I was in the underworld. Will they be angry with me?"

Oka'ra shook his head. "No, I believe you were sent there to rescue the child. If he is one of theirs, they will come for him."

"Should we worry?" Someone asked.

"We must honor the gods." Oka'ra replied. "In six days time, the moon will be full. On that night, we will offer our thanks to the gods, and give the child a name. If the thunders hear our prayers, they will come."

CHAPTER FORTY-THREE

"Bring the firewood over here," one of the elders said. "I am too old to be walking all that way for a few twigs."

Akhila stood aside while two young boys gathered up the pile of wood and brought it closer to the old woman. She laughed out loud and shook her head. The longhouses had been bustling with activity the whole week preparing for the full moon. The prospect of *actual* thunders visiting her community was both daunting and exciting. After all she had seen in the last eleven months, Akhila seemed to be the only one in the tribe who wasn't nervous.

As the last rays of sunlight disappeared on the horizon, the community fire was lit. Then the tribe's strongest warriors, dressed in their ceremonial garb, began pounding out an elaborate dance around the fire while the sound of a dozen water drums carried the songs sung by the clan-mothers to the ears of the gods.

At the entrance of the chief's longhouse, crouched Oka'ra, the seer of visions, dressed only in a pair of long leather britches and donning his red and black false face mask. Beside him, leaning against a tree was Balthazar, wrapped snugly on a fur lined cradle board. As the drums went silent and the dancing stopped, he raised his hands to the sky.

"Hinon has blessed our clan with another bountiful

year," Oka'ra began, "we thank you creator, for helping us to keep our belly's full in the coming winter."

Oka'ra paused, peering out through the eye holes in his mask to see the leaders of the tribe nod in agreement.

"Now, in thankfulness, we present to you this child," he continued, "saved from the creatures of the land of the dead by one of our own."

The shaman reached down and picked up baby Balthazar.

"Bonsari," he said, "have the clan-mothers chosen a name for the boy?"

"Yes," she replied, stepping forward. "His name is Otkon Ori:te',"

She reached out her finger, and gently ran it down the center of Balthazar's face, leaving a line of red paint from the center of his eyebrows down the length of his nose. Then she tucked strand of beads down in the wraps of his cradle board and stepped back.

Oka'ra nodded in approval and lifted the child up over his head.

"Great Hinon," he called out, "we offer you this child. Show us the destiny you have planned for him, the one we now call 'Spirit Dove'."

On his last word, a bright light streamed down from the heavens, illuminating the village like the midday sun. The clouds parted overhead, revealing two winged beings descending into the center of the clearing. They were dressed in simple clothes: tunic, long britches and moccasins which all glowed with a light that seemed to come from within the being wearing them.

"Your prayers have been heard," one of the beings

said.

As the whole tribe dropped down onto one knee, the other being stepped toward the fire and addressed them.

"Which of you is Akhila, Mermaid of the Flint Place?" he asked.

"I am," Akhila answered stepping forward.

"My name is Nuriel and this is my brother, Baracheil," the being said. "I have been most anxious to meet you."

Akhila's brow pulled down into a frown.

"Why is that?" she asked.

"Because without your help, the power of the Orcus Child would have fallen into the hands of evil forces." Nuriel said. "But because you listened, he has been spared."

"And now," Baracheil said, "It is time for us to take the child."

Akhila looked over Nuriel's shoulder at the baby in Oka'ra's hands. She reached up and wiped away a tear.

"Must you take him?" Oka'ra asked.

"I am afraid so," Baracheil said gently removing the child from the shaman's hands. "Otkon Ori:te' has a very important job to do."

Nuriel and Baracheil both extended their wings and slowly began ascending into the night sky. When the two had reached the tops of the trees, they hovered there for just a moment.

"Akhila," Baracheil called out.

"I am here," she responded.

"Do not despair about the child," he said, "Your path and his will cross again, someday."

On his last word, another beam of light streamed

down from the heavens and in that moment, they were gone.

Tsio wrapped his arms around Akhila.

"It sounds as though you too will have an important job to do."

"I hope so," she sighed.

THE END

ACKNOWLEDGMENTS

What a magical and wondrous world we live in. A place filled with endless creativity, given to us in stewardship so many millennia ago. Those who take that position seriously, are true treasures on this earth.

While those treasures are many, there is one community who honored this book beyond measure. The Kontewinneh'a:we Akwesasne Women Singers truly blessed me with their beautiful serenade: "Water Song," written by Theresa "Bear" Fox. These ladies continue to practice the priceless traditions of the Mohawk Nation as "Carriers of the Words," ensuring that their language and culture will echo through eternity. I am humbled beyond measure to include that tradition in this book.

Follow The Kontewinneh'a:we Akwesasne Women Singers on Facebook:
https://www.facebook.com/kontiwennenhawi/

And listen to the voices of these talented ladies on YouTube:
https://youtu.be/9MvNaFWcQf4?list=RD5ei4CQWCP4c

www.ingramcontent.com/pod-product-compliance
Lightning Source LLC
Chambersburg PA
CBHW020803190726
48285CB00006B/2153